TANNENBAUM ARMS

DARLENE WESENBERG RZEZOTARSKI

Created with Vellum

TANNENBAUM ARMS

Wecker Press

Darlene Wesenberg Rzezotarski

"In the end, what saves the past is the stories we tell about it. It is our stories that take dead objects and boring documents and make them live again."

William Cronin

This book is dedicated to C. George Rzezotarski, diligent local historian, whose collection of documents from the sixties and early seventies enabled the poet in me to anchor her tale.

ACKNOWLEDGEMENTS

A wave to my writing group who encouraged me from the beginning: Carla Luna Cullen, Rufina Garay, Shlomo Levin, Lisa Minetti, Jenny Motl, and Virginia Small;

A hug to Janine Arseneau, writing cohort from Woodland Pattern;

A nod to editor Vince Bushell who encouraged the resurrection of this novel and published it monthly in *Riverwest Currents* from April, 2022, to January, 2023;

A bow to Alexander McCall Smith whose writers' challenge launched this venture.

All good....
DWRZ

DISCLAIMER:

Although many actual individuals, events and locations are referenced, this remains a work of fiction, informed by life experience. The main characters emerged from my brain after a frightful headache, fully clothed in their suits of armor.

CHAPTER 1

SEPTEMBER 1969

Wherein late bloomers Lily Swan and Joshua (Blue Jay) Haakens become caretakers of a six-family apartment building just two blocks from the University of Wisconsin-Milwaukee campus where both are students. They decide to inhabit the somewhat musty basement apartment where they are given the opportunity to live rent-free in exchange for cleaning the halls, tending the boiler, and renting vacant units.

You'd never know it was September, the way the sun beat down. And you'd never know that the young man and woman pausing in the middle of the sidewalk in front of the red brick building were anything other than random passers-by. If you looked a bit closer, what seemed a navy-blue backpack was actually a canvas and aluminum back carrier with a baby nestling in it.

They blended in with the university area crowd—she with her walnut-brown hair parted in the middle and hanging straight below her shoulders, he with his red curls bursting out of his scalp like a white-boy Afro, both wearing various shades of denim.

"Well, the building looks solid enough to me," the young man observed. "No excess anything. Just a straightforward building. Not much grass to cut, considering it's on a corner. Pseudo-grand main entryway, tall enough for giants to pass through without stooping. Tannenbaum Arms. Where'd they come up with that name? Six mailboxes. Carpeted stairway visible through the glass. Looks like it goes up all three floors, two apartments on each floor. I don't think we're expected to do windows."

"It doesn't look like anybody ever does windows."

The young woman grabbed the foot of the red-headed child she bore on her back, a miniature version of the young man, but naked except for a diaper and a necklace with jingle

bells and beads. "Hey, Hatchling!" She tickled his toes through his sock. "Whaddaya think, Blue Jay? Shall we just keep walking?"

He tugged at her sleeve. "C'mon, Lily! Let's go for it! Let's not mention that we have a dog, okay?"

"By the way, do you see The Hatchling's moccasin anywhere? I wonder where he lost it."

Because of the oppressive heat, it was almost a pleasure for Lily and Blue Jay to walk down the five musty concrete steps at the rear of the building to the cooler lower level for their interview with the property representative. The apartment had been referred to in the classified ad as an "English Basement Apartment," creating the image of geraniums and crisp criss-crossed curtains and respite from a bustling city scene. In reality, this definitely was a Wisconsin basement--damp, with small windows running the length of the building overlooking another building twelve feet away—except for the front, where the two windows might prove great for viewing the shoes of anyone passing by on the sidewalk. And it felt so cool—almost like air conditioning.

Because it was September, classes were about to start at the university where Lily was beginning a master's degree in sociology and Blue Jay, about five years belatedly, was finishing his bachelor's degree in English. The idea of a building caretakership was Lily's bright idea after talking to a friend at the Well Baby Free Clinic, and she forged ahead with glib-tongued determination.

Their appointment with the property manager seemed to be going well as they moved through the apartment. After introducing himself and shaking hands with Jay, making momentary eye contact with a forced smile never leaving his face, Mr. Gerhart Dreschler kept a respectful distance from them, as if his tweed sports jacket might suddenly sprout a peace button on its lapel if he got too close. His well-trimmed hair seemed glued to his scalp—was that hair tonic or sweat? —and he kept checking his watch.

"Yes, Mr. Dreschler, we're fully trained boiler operators," Lily asserted. "We apprenticed with the Werners down the street." She gave a warning glance to Blue Jay. Actually, they were trained in nothing, but her baby clinic friend had a friend who was a genuine building super who had said they could use him as a reference. This was a matter of urgency precluding honest responses. Finances were tight, with a combination of scholarships, work-study jobs, student loans, and occasional trips to a blood center, which offered cash for their rare O Negative blood.

As they walked through the hall, Lily pondered, "How can he wear that wooly jacket in this weather?" She was prone to interior philosophizing, even under tense circumstances:

"Clothing really makes a personal statement. *Twixt Tweed and Denim*. It could be an impressively large coffee table book emphasizing the generation gap. We could have a picture of Jay standing next to Mr. Dreschler on the cover. Trendy bell bottoms next to wool trousers with razor-sharp creases...."

She pulled herself back to reality as the tour continued. "Jay, this could be The Hatchling's room. It would be quiet here off the kitchen. And there in the front under the porch, that could be our study. What do you think? If you need a break from studying, you can always have the view of the sidewalk."

The apartment had the unmistakable aura and odor of basement, yet it was spacious, with worn wood floors running the entire length of the east side of the building. The boiler pipes decorated the ceiling but were high enough that no one would have to stoop to get past them. Out the windows, perhaps ten feet away, one could peer into the utility rooms of the neighboring building. "I could talk myself into this, maybe hang a spider plant from the pipes in the kitchen," Lily thought out loud, taking one final look around before leaving the living area. Under her breath, she added, "Free rent!"

They crossed a small courtyard beneath the fire escape and entered the laundry room. "Here's a bonus," said Mr. Dreschler. "You are allowed to mark five dollars in quarters with red nail polish for your laundry at these pay machines. When the maintenance people come at the end of every month, your marked quarters will be returned to you. In exchange, you are expected to keep this laundry room in tip-top condition."

"That seems doable!" Lily said, eyeing the moldy-looking floors that seemed not to have been touched in years. "Just get me some bleach and I'll shape this up in no time."

She had been insistent on using cloth diapers, necessitating frequent pilgrimages to a laundromat, so the vision of nearby washers and a pocketful of gleaming red quarters floated like a beckoning angel.

Blue Jay reinforced their air of expertise when the grand tour proceeded across the walkway, past storage bins, to the adjacent boiler room that ran the length of the street side of the building. "Ah, yes!" he smiled knowingly. "You have a Kewaunee boiler!" tapping its side like it was his long-lost friend.

The boiler was an awesome spectacle, rusted in places, with metal patches where there must have been leaks, pipes branching out in all directions like the rays a metal octopus. Jay thought it looked to be a hundred years old. In the far corner was a dingy room that must have once been a coal bin. Jay figured that was the source of the sour smell permeating the lower level.

Lily knew from talking to Ernie Werner, the obliging building super on the next corner, that the important safety measure would be to check the balance of steam and water level in the glass gauge on the side at least twice a day when the boiler was running. Obviously, the boiler was not turned on at this time, and the gauge itself looked filled with rust. The whole thing looked like it needed to be relocated in a dump and nobody would miss it. For a moment, Lily pictured the building exploding in a Vesuvius of steam and had second thoughts. She exchanged a glance with Jay. Reassured by his broad grin, she held her tongue.

Mr. Dreschler looked them over, glancing curiously at the baby boy that Lily was wearing in a contraption on her back, and paused.

Their future financial lives hung in his gaze. Lily surmised that they looked like refugees from another world from the perspective of this gentleman in his well-tailored jacket, this expertly coifed man accustomed to those hand-rolled cigars bulging in his shirt pocket—but she need not have worried. "You sound knowledgeable, and most people don't want to live in an English basement." He hesitated, "Oh, not that it isn't cool in summer and warm in winter, being half underground." He then offered a further gesture of intimacy and friendship. He lowered his voice. "I had to evict the last caretakers for drunkenness. They seemed okay, but they couldn't hold their liquor. Tenants started calling me directly at all hours of the night."

Jay smiled, "Well, you don't have to worry about us with that problem."

He continued, "Be prepared for occasional flare-ups. That's only normal in the caretaking business. This building used to be all sedate older people, but now it's a mix of all types. The neighborhood is changing, and we can't leave units vacant too long looking for Mr. and Mrs. Perfection. You'll have to work out relationships on your own. I don't want to be bothered with their squabbles."

Lily quickly picked up the conversation, thinking it best to change the subject. "By the way, this is our son Joshua Peregrine."

Mr. Dreshler nodded, "Peregrine? As in pilgrim?"

"No. Peregrine, as in falcon. He's three months old now," she added, hoping that would work in their favor. "Christmas Day will be his half birthday." She babbled on. "Blue Jay and Falcon. Birds, you see. That's why we call him The Hatchling."

He smiled dismissively at Lily and nodded at Blue Jay. "That's a fine little boy you've got there. Are you a Wisconsin boy yourself?"

Blue Jay shook his head, "Well, almost. That is, I've lived here the past six years. I'm actually a Yooper."

Mr. Dreschler looked puzzled and raised his eyebrows in an expression that Jay interpreted as alarm. "A Yippie?"

"No, a Yooper. That's what we Upper Peninsula Michigan

folks call ourselves." He paused. "As opposed to city slicker, you know." This was Jay's attempt at a joke. "I traded Lake Superior for Lake Michigan."

Mr. Dreschler hesitated, as if swallowing this rare tidbit of information. "If you're really interested in this caretaking business, I think we can work something out. Free rent and eighty dollars a month. You keep the cleaning supplies stocked. Keep the building clean, the snow shoveled, the grass cut, the tenants happy. Also, show any vacant units. I make the final decision on rental, but I take your judgment into account. At present the units are all filled. Agreed?"

Lily and Blue Jay nodded at each other. "Agreed." Their sighs were audible.

Mr. Dreschler extended his hand, first to Lily and then again to Blue Jay. They solemnly shook hands.

"When would you be able to start, assuming you pass the background check?"

"Well, we could move next weekend," Lily said, trying not to appear too eager, visions of extra money dancing behind her green eyes.

They walked him to the front of the building and watched as he pulled away in his gleaming black Buick.

"Let's walk around the building and have a look out here," Jay suggested.

"Sure. And then let's go to the Ben Franklin and buy red nail polish!"

THE SEMESTER BEGAN three days before they moved. They borrowed a car from a member of Jay's poetry group, rented a U-Haul, said a happy goodbye to the one-room efficiency over a head shop on the Lower East Side, and packed and lugged and juggled baby care and classes. The not-so-trivial matter of the boiler operator's license would have to be faced soon enough. Classes had started and moving, studying, and settling in was an all-consuming task, not to mention that The Hatchling was off his feed in this new place and was waking up nightly around 2:00 AM ready for action.

Lily drifted through the days in half-sleep. "At least this place doesn't reek of patchouli oil seeping in through the floor-boards. Don't worry about the boiler operator license. It's a long time before it's gonna be cold enough to turn on the rusty drag-on," she advised Blue Jay

Boiler procrastination was fine with him. He was already begun composing a lengthy poetic drama, *The Tragedie of Joanie Fist*, for his advanced creative writing class, in addition to his other sixteen credits. "Ich spreche Deutsch!" he said aloud, then cleared his throat and repeated the phrase with an exaggerated guttural sound on the letter R. "Ich Spgrgrgrgreche Deutsch!" He sighed, a bit insecure about his latest attempt at linguistic acquisition, a required six credits of a foreign language for the liberal arts diploma—three per semester. He had dropped a Spanish class during his sophomore year, showing little apti-tude for foreign tongues. Now he needed the German class to fulfill the requirement before his targeted June graduation. "June!" he smiled to himself. "Just around the corner. Sure."

Six years of student loans were piling up. Graduating in June had become urgent and serious since the birth of his son; although he was the type of person who could have remained a perpetual student, could have been happy, happy, happy as a raven, evermore. Of course, perpetual student hood was no longer an option.

~

On Monday morning after the weekend move, Lily posted a handwritten notice beside the mailboxes in the front hall:

Notice to the Tenants of Tannenbaum Arms:

This is a message from your new caretakers. We live in the English Basement apartment across from the laundry room. We are students at UWM and have arranged our class schedules so one of us will be in residence at all times. Please leave a message in the box by our door to notify us of any special building concerns. In case of a building emergency, please call us. As soon as we get a phone, we will post the number. (Of course, if it is a serious emergency, just call the fire department or police department, which is just what we would do anyway.) Our son Joshua usually naps between 1 and 3 PM when we are lucky, so please do not disturb during those hours unless you are reporting an emergency. We try to get him to sleep by 7. We look forward to meeting all of you and taking care of this building.

All the best for good days in a good place,

Lily and Joshua, AKA Blue Jay

As she was standing back to admire her work, a tall woman who looked as old as Mother Time herself came walking up the front steps, propping herself with two canes, the handles of a bulging shopping bag looped through her right arm. Her gray hair was pulled back in a neat bun and she wore a gray sweater to match.

Lily stepped forward to hold the door open and reached for the bag to help her.

A look of disdain came over the woman's face and she raised her cane at Lily, as if to strike her.

"No, thank you! I can take care of myself," she half snarled.

"Well, sure," Lily said. "You must be one of the tenants. "I'm Lily and I'm half the team of your new building caretakers."

"Pleased to meet you." She paused and forced a little smile. "I'm Mrs. Davis. Mabel Davis. Apartment 4. And now I must be on my way. As you can see, I'm carrying quite a load here, and I don't want my ice cream to melt." She made circles in the air with her cane, waving it in Lily's direction.

"Yes, I have to get back downstairs anyway. I left my son in his crib. You might want to read the notice when you're not so loaded down," Lily said, stepping out through the door and almost skipping around to the back.

"Well, Hatchling," she said when she returned to their lower level, "isn't it super, being a super! Did you know that your mommy is a super-duper super? And Mrs. Davis is so-o-o friendly!"

Blue Jay had made it a habit to take an early morning walk this canine pre-nuptial contribution to their union. Procured during his Poe-infatuation Phase, Lost Lenore was a Humane Society dog of indeterminate origin—perhaps some mixture of beagle and poodle, with a little goat thrown in. (The beagle part would account for the floppy ears, black spots, and talent for putting her head back and howling at the sound of every siren, no matter how distant. Further speculation informed them that a poodle ancestor might have given her the wiry coat, and somewhere back in the lineage, a remote goat had instilled a penchant for chewing all pillows and shoes left near her nose.) "She's fifty-seven varieties, just like every other red-blooded American," Blue Jay had pontificated. "Why should our dog be any different from the rest of us?"

On the first day in their new apartment, before leaving for class, Jay took The Hatchling and the bounding beast on a quick morning constitutional. A block away, he ran into two people, one of them vaguely recalled from last spring's European History class, but who now wore his hair long and sported a chest full of protest buttons. "Jay, Man! Remember me? Peter Thomas. We're meeting tonight at the fountain for a little action."

Lenore tugged at her leash, eager to move on. Jay shrugged.

"They're trying to impose a curfew, but this won't happen. It's a revolution. We won't be fucked with!" he continued. "A little bit of Chicago in Milwaukee, but pigs are pigs."

"I had enough of Chicago in Chicago, Pete," Jay countered. He pushed back recent disturbing memories.

Lost Lenore tried to jump up and lick Pete's face, but Jay pulled her back.

"This here is my friend, Krazy Wayne."

The bespectacled man in the army jacket covered with peace signs nodded. "It will be a night to remember." Lenore tried to embrace him, "Whoa, Beast! Maybe leave your dog home, Dude."

"Krazy Wayne earned the stripes on that jacket. He served in Nam, but he came home hating that hell hole," Pete continued.

Krazy Wayne bowed mechanically three times and squinted, reminding Blue Jay of the movements of a cartoon character. "I'd rather not talk about it right now. Almost got ground up in the big meat chopper. Lost too many brothers. Up with the fuckin' revolution!" he rasped, his voice taking on a noticeable edge. Abruptly, his temperament changed as he focused on The Hatchling. "Looks like you took the married-student-fatherhood route to dodge the draft. Not too shitty, except it'll take eighteen years to get out of that deal."

At this change of tone and attention to her human baby

brother, Lenore's hair began to stand on end. Jay pulled hard on her leash, backing off.

"Uncle Sam doesn't care about my paternity. Up with academia and down with Lost Lenore. Time for me to get back to work. Can't make it this time," Jay shrugged, remembering how just a couple years before, the gathering place around the fountain next to the tall water tower was a place people could actually go to for respite. He and Lily used to sit there and gaze out at Lake Michigan and contemplate the fate of the cosmos. Lily had made up a story about a wizard living in the water tower, looking out protectively over the East Side. Now this park had become a small battleground. "What happened to the wizard?" Jay checked himself as he almost spoke these words out loud.

"Peace, brother!" And they continued on their way.

When Jay returned, he did not mention this meeting to Lily. The activities around the fountain had begun to escalate nightly, but there was enough to deal with right here, even more than enough. Even too much. Let this phase of the revolution be fought outside their small domain, was his opinion. He embraced Lily in a big bear hug, grabbed his backpack, and was off to class. "Here's hoping for a quiet afternoon."

As he walked the five blocks to campus, his thoughts went back to his dues paid marching on the raucous streets of Chicago during the 1968 Democratic Convention. "A nightmare of societal break-down, all the way around," he thought. "Worthy of a poem, but how to express the indignation and taunts and rocks of the protesters, the indiscriminate clubbing by officers going into blind rage, the helicopters hovering overhead like noisy pterodactyls. The fear of death by drubbing." He paused near campus and contemplated some cumulous clouds with dark underbellies breezily sailing along towards Lake Michigan. "I need to get back to Grant Park someday," he mused, "to see it again, to get over the memory of being blinded by teargas and crawling along on the grass like a centipede to hide in some bushes." The germs of a new poem infected his brain.

~

"Dress the Hatchling, leash up Lenore, walk them both, buy some food, unpack some boxes, find my Psych text, feed the Hatchling, read the assignment, line up supper, get ready for class...." Lily sang the morning agenda as she pulled the child from his baby seat and spun him around in a little dance.

Aside from the fact that she couldn't find a book required for her Population and Social Interaction course, therefore could not do her homework, the morning passed exactly as planned. The tenants seemed to be sequestered in their quarters; and the sky, not visible through the windows of their basement apartment, began to darken into rain. "I can get used to this," she thought. The ground itself was ear-level, and as raindrops splashed and splattered outside, they created an unlikely symphony of water-weather sounds. She snuggled next to The Hatchling on the big bed and was lulled into dreamless sleep.

At noon, Blue Jay trotted through the door and was greeted with a quick kiss and a few words: "Be sure to hang around for the phone man and do some unpacking if you can.

We still have a mess here. Let me know if you run across the Ehrlich book, *The Population Bomb*. It has a gray cover with dire messages about dead babies on it. It's got to be around here somewhere. I'm supposed to have it read by next week."

Blue Jay threw his soggy jacket over a kitchen chair. Lost Lenore bounded up to him as he sat. "It's raining cats and DOGS, Lenore! Dogs!"

"Oh, and I made you a ham sandwich, and there's orange banana Jello in the fridge. Love you!"

Lily grabbed her umbrella and sloshed her way to the university.

Blue Jay propped his book on the table, hoping to cover a chapter before The Hatchling would wake up.

In theory, beginning on this day with their boxes almost all unpacked and the building set to right, life was to settle into a routine. Blue Jay had scheduled his classes for the morning, since he was a morning person; Lily had the afternoon slot, except for her "Impact of Puritan Morality on American Society" seminar, which met Wednesday evenings. In theory....

Wednesday afternoon began serenely enough. Blue Jay snuggled The Hatchling in his arms and sang him poems from Blake's *Songs of Innocence and Experience,* until The Hatchling fell asleep in the midst of "Little Lamb, Who Made Thee?" Ever so carefully, Blue Jay carried his little bundle into the nursery off the kitchen and gave a silent cheer as his son remained asleep. Retreating to his study, Blue Jay resumed work on *The Tragedie of Joanie Fist.*

Both father and son were jarred back to reality by the urgent ringing of the doorbell, which resounded from some undisclosed location deep within the anteroom, its harsh ring more like the alarm on an elevator stuck between floors than a self-respecting English Basement domicile's doorbell.

"Yes?" Blue Jay called, rushing to the door.

"It's just me. Moisette from Apartment 5. I'm locked out. I'm wondering if you have a key...." She stood in the doorway, her love beads hanging to her waist, her black dress clinging to her from the rain, which had already moved out over the lake.

"Well, sure. Hang on." He grabbed an impressive bunch of keys from the kitchen table. "C'mon in while I find out how to do this. You're the first one to need a key." Since the doorbell had awakened The Hatchling, Blue Jay picked him up and unceremoniously put the screaming child into his bouncy seat, as he ruminated over the keys. Mr. Dreschler had not informed them about which key went to what, although they had noted that the apartment keys were double-locked in a metal box in the anteroom, just next to the fuses.

The Lost Lenore, having heard the commotion, roused herself from her spot on the front windowsill and scampered in, greeting Moisette as a long-lost friend.

"Your dog is very presumptuous. It assumes I want to be kissed."

"Sorry."

"Well, kisses can be wonderful, but not from a dog." In a manner she was sure many admirers perceived to be coy and winsome, she smiled at Blue Jay, who didn't notice. "My hair is a little soaked from that cloudburst. Sorry if I am not presenting my best image." She shook her head, sending her mass of dark strands swirling in all directions.

"Sorry. Down, Lenore."

The dog reluctantly backed off.

"She thinks everybody loves her."

"Well, I've always been a cat person. In fact, some people say I resemble a cat, with my slanted sloe eyes." She smiled at him, edging closer. "What do you think?"

"I think I better go check for your keys before The Hatchling gets hungry. You know these babies. Always demanding something. Milk. Burping. Diaper duty. Biscuit break. German lessons," he began ad-libbing as he tried various keys. "Bingo!" He opened the case. "What apartment did you say you were in?"

She sighed in mock frustration, "Apartment 5. At least the rain stopped. Come up for a drink whenever you need a break from the baby-and-dog scene. We're all grown-ups living up there." With a toss of her head and a wink of her eye, she flounced out into the musty hallway.

He handed her the key. "Thanks. Just shove this key under the back door when you're done. I'm going to have to get The Hatchling to sleep again so I can get some work done." He gestured to the random cardboard boxes around the kitchen.

Moisette stood in the doorway, "Doesn't he have a civilized name?"

At that point, Lenore saw her chance to make a getaway and streaked past Moisette, bounded up the steps, and disappeared.

"Well, isn't that the cat's meow?" laughed Moisette, slinking away up the basement steps and disappearing around to the front of the building.

BLUE JAY REACHED for The Hatchling and the dog leash in one fell swoop and ran outside calling for Lenore, who was arching her back on the neighbor's lawn, leaving a generous deposit of potential fertilizer. Just then, a woman flew out, camera in hand. "Get that dog off my grass! Immediately!"

"Ma'am, I'm trying to do that. Never mind. I'm your new neighbor. I'll get it cleaned up, but first I have to catch her before she's hit by a car. She has no street sense."

"Immediately! I'm calling the police!"

"This whole world has gone insane," he thought. He made a lunge for Lenore, snagging her by her rear right paw as she attempted to flee. "Good dog. Great dog. Wonderful dog!" he crooned. Riding under his father's left arm like a sack of flour, the Hatchling, thinking this was a great game, began to gurgle in a deep-throated, wide-awake way.

"Yeah, this is a new game. Catch-the-Pup, to be followed by Clean-the-Poop," said Blue Jay.

Back in the apartment, The Hatchling was once again lulled to sleep and Blue Jay, forgetting about Lenore's deposit on the neighbor's manicured lawn, began to focus on outlining his semester-long creative writing class project, a blank verse drama, *The Tragedie of Joanie Fist*. Since it had begun as a contemporary re-interpretation of Goethe's *Tragedy of Johann Faust*, Jay debated adding a scene about the death of the Old Society, which had sold its soul to the devil, replaced by a New Age of love and peace; but that no longer rang true. Although he had been busy making ends meet on the night shift at a Stop and Shop Market and could not go to Woodstock the past summer, he wanted to incorporate the notion in his play that 70,000 people could peacefully enjoy one another's company with mud and music; but only one week before Woodstock, on the other coast, a pregnant movie star, Sharon Tate, and her friends living in a Hollywood mansion were brutally stabbed to death and the word PIG written in her blood. How could he encompass this vastness of good and evil within the human heart with his poetic drama? He lost himself in contemplation.

Five minutes later, the doorbell rang. The Hatchling began whimpering in his crib. A voice called out, "Telephone Man!" A second, sterner voice called out, "Police!"

"Well," thought Blue Jay, "maybe it will take a few days for things to fall into a routine."

It turned out that the nephew of the neighbor was a police officer who was perhaps overstepping his duty when he issued a warning ticket to Blue Jay, who somewhat belatedly located a plastic bread bag and a spatula and went to clean up Lenore's offering of fertilizer. The telephone man was not at all fazed by sharing his visit, and all went well with the installation of the device that was to prove itself a total nuisance over the next several months by ringing at all the wrong times.

As evening settled in, after a brief time at home, Lily hiked up to campus for the first meeting of her Wednesday seminar, which meant that Blue Jay was eating supper with The Hatchling, who thought that getting mashed peas and apple sauce all over his face was great fun, especially when he could make a bubbly gurgling sound with it. Blue Jay ruminated over his elegant supper of peanut butter and jelly sandwich and tall glass of milk--which, the ads assured him, had been produced from contented cows. A song came on the radio—something about a woman named Suzanne who had a supply of tea and oranges from China. Blue Jay stopped in mid-chew and turned up the volume. Tea and oranges certainly was more poetic than milk and peanut butter. The voice sounded rather cow-like, but the words! This was poetry set to music, not music with a rhyme thrown in! This was an amazing poet!

The DJ's voice came on as the music faded. "This is Bob Reitman, WUWM-FM, playing favorites, starting with the title cut from the 1968 album by Leonard Cohen of Montreal, Canada...."

As Reitman announced the next Cohen song from his new album, *Bird on a Wire*, Blue Jay asked himself, "Where have I been for two years? Buried in my great night shift at Stop and Shop with Muzak, or with books and babies. Or baby." He resolved to duck into a listening booth at Schroeder's Books and Records for a full album listening session as soon as he had a chance.

Perhaps they should go to Canada, he thought. Then imagine... life skipping out on student loans, without burning draft cards, without a Vietnam Undeclared War, without student strikes and sit-ins and without police teargassing taunting

Yippies .... "Let's see. We take our student loan money, and instead of paying the tuition, we simply get on a train and go to Montreal. We find out where this musician lives and we knock on his door. 'Hello, Mr. Cohen. We are political refugees. No, we are poetical refugees from Milwaukee, USA. Can we please camp in your back yard? What? You're just going on a concert tour? What a coincidence. My wife and I are trained in property management. We are a team. Fifty-fifty. Do you have a boiler? We could take care of your house while you're gone. What? You're just borrowing this pad from a friend? Oh...."

So much for that idea. Even his daydreams took a realistic twist these days. "Hey, squawky Hatchling, how about going on a little stroll?" This was a well-known technique for putting the child to sleep, leaving Blue Jay with a long evening for further contemplation and, quite possibly, some studying.

At ten PM Lily came home, too tired to talk. By 10:05, she had kicked her sandals off and was brushing her teeth. The doorbell rang. "Get it, Jay," she effervesced through the toothpaste.

"Can't you get it? I'm half naked."

"Oh, great," she stomped to the door. "Yes?"

"Hi. I'm Craig from Apartment 6. I'm locked out."

"I'm your caretaker. I'm rabid and foaming at the mouth. I'm insane. Lemme get you a key."

Craig stood there not knowing if he should laugh or run. He had played football in high school, but now that he was a college student, he preferred the drinking team and proudly wore his expanding six-pack stomach, which tonight hung over his jeans like the hangover he'd have the next morning. "I'm sorry to disturb you," he mumbled, as she came forward with the key. He lifted his right hand in a V sign, while attempting to twirl the keys in his left. "Peace!"

"It's okay. Just shove it under our door after you let yourself in," she gurgled. "Don't stumble. Maybe use the front stairs, not the fire escape tonight," she couldn't help adding, noticing his somewhat inebriated condition.

She rinsed her mouth. "That's it. No more interruptions. Let's post a note that we do not answer doorbells after 9 PM. This job could eat us up if we let it."

When Lily got like this, sometimes the best tactic was diversion. He reached for her, putting his arm around her and pulling her close. "Hey, I heard this great song on the radio. Leonard Cohen. Canadian poet. Wanna move to Canada?"

"Yeah, sure. Along with everyone else playing draft dodgeball and their cousin. Leonard Schmeonard. This is home. Even if I hate what the country is doing with Nixon's damn war, I'm red-blooded. They can't get rid of me that fast. I prefer Hendrix twanging out 'The Star Spangled Banner.' Anyway, it was a long day. I'm too tired to talk."

" I have a solution for that," Jay countered. "Let's hit the feathers."

THEIR CLASS SCHEDULES seemed to be moving along and the semester began to take on a life of its own. It looked as if the tenants were all quite reasonable with their demands. Craig introduced a new roommate in Apartment Six, a transfer student from Cleveland named Joe who figured out after two weeks that he couldn't take dorm life. He and Craig were off to a protest at the new Performing Arts Center, hoping to disrupt the grand opening. "All the big shots will be there," Joe proclaimed. "Tickets are $100 apiece. What normal person could afford that?"

Craig flashed a poster: "Down With Fat Cats, Up with People." He grinned. "Ready for the outside show."

Jay and Lily declined an invitation to join them, with growing awareness that opportunities for protest would be constant.

Near the end of the month, the Students for a Democratic Society confronted the ROTC program on campus, believing this military group had no place on campus. The afternoon classes in Bolton Hall were disrupted by a parade of protestors making their way through the halls. Lily heard the chants from her second-floor classroom.

"One, two, three, four, We don't want yer fuckin' war!" competed with the professor's drone, and disheartened students stopped taking notes.

Looking around the room, the professor sighed and said, "You may use the rest of the period to work on your assignments independently. Class dismissed."

"Good that I have afternoons and Jay has mornings," Lily remarked to her friend and fellow student Pam as they left the room. This semester they had this statistics class together and managed to save seats for each other. "Jay would be joining the marchers by now, I'm sure. But I think we will go on the protest march this weekend, just walking from UWM to the War Museum. It should be non-violent enough to deal with and I want my voice to be heard. Well, maybe not heard, but I want to be present. You know. Bearing witness. Nixon has it really wrong."

Pam shrugged. "Tough all the way around. Damned if you do; damned if you don't." Since meeting Pam last spring in a Sociology of Education class when she was juggling the end of the semester and advanced pregnancy, Lily was relieved to find a friend she could relate to openly, who could be counted on to understand her situation. "You should switch to a practical master's like me," she advised. "Education. Always a job in that market. That means, a paycheck. What will you ever do with that degree in Sociology? Go on for another degree, and then another, and then what?"

Lily realized that Pam had an opinion on everything and knew when to just laugh; although she thought perhaps Pam was making a good argument in favor of an education degree.

Class had been dismissed twenty minutes early, so they walked to the Union for coffee and rare conversation time. Pam was a single parent. She had a two-year-old daughter who was truly in her terrible twos. Her mother was assisting her with childcare. "You get to look forward to acting-out behavior with Little Jay," she said. "It can't be helped. And the way people are conducting themselves, there is way too much acting out for me."

Lily laughed. "Well, I keep my *Dr. Spock Baby Book* handy. I think Little Jay is right on target for almost four months. He likes to smile and put things in this mouth and drop food off his tray."

The corridor was littered with upturned trashcans and chairs. They stepped cautiously. They crossed the mall, littered with protest flyers and more overturned trash cans and benches, making their way to the student union.

"Damn this useless mess. I think I need a brownie and goop," Pam stated, referring to a favorite campus treat consisting of a large slab of a very chewy chocolate brownie with an added swirl of ice milk from a dispenser. "A little sweetness to temper all the bitterness flowing through the air." The near-empty dining hall seemed a surprising island of tranquility.

"Good that they didn't drain the goop machine," Pam remarked. They plopped down at a nearby table absorbing the clatter and hum of the cafeteria that surrounded them, blocking out all thoughts of war, discussing the challenges of motherhood.

"I heard a rumor. There is a possibility of establishing a drop-off daycare center for students with young children. I would be happy to work there a few hours in exchange for Molly getting to stay there when I'm in class. I hate listening to my mom's self-righteous martyrdom. She loves Molly, but she says she already raised me and my brother and that was enough. She only half means it, but I get the point."

"Maybe she just wants to be appreciated," Lily remarked. "But you know, according to Spock, daycare could help the children socialize with each other. Learn to get along, and all. I was just reading about that."

"Molly could use a little socialization. Sorry to say, she bit her three-year-old cousin for grabbing her favorite bear. No harm done. No tooth marks. Lesson learned, I hope."

Both women shared a laugh over this.

"Keep me posted if you hear anything, Pam." Lily scraped the last bit of chocolate from her bowl. "I better run. I have the evening shift tonight. Jay has a poetry group and I have trash duty at Tannenbaum Arms."

CHAPTER 2
OCTOBER

Wherein Lily and Blue Jay become better acquainted with their tenants, acquire their boiler operator's licenses; and through a cluster of unplanned events, discover that the secret of striving for normalcy is to admit that there is no normalcy.

In early October, it began to get a bit chilly when the damp winds blew in from Lake Michigan. Lily checked out a thick book, *Bailey's Boiler Handbook,* from the library and got a study guide from the Milwaukee Department of Building Inspection. Soon they must face up to their shortcomings. The operation of a large boiler like the Kewaunee was a very responsible job, and she wanted to be able to do her best so as not to explode the building or cause some terrible meltdown. Secretly, she regretted getting them into this position, but decided to put on a brave face and take the challenge. After all, she reasoned, most boiler operators were not college grads who had honed their test-taking skills over sixteen or more years in the educational system. The hand-out from the city said to bring a #2 lead pencil, indicating some kind of objective answers. Actually, on the job all they would have to do is check the water level on the glass gauge, keep the boiler properly filled, and control the thermostat which was conveniently located in the central hallway of their basement apartment. And, of course, in case of boiler failure they just had to call Mr. Dreschler.

After a heated discussion about the boiler, it was decided that Lily would take the test first. She pored over the overdue *Bailey's Boiler Handbook* and taught herself how to compute the steam compression, the rate of pressure needed to heat a three-story building, and how thick the uptake pipes needed to be to convey the necessary pressure effectively. Although this crash course on boilers put her behind in her academics, she confidently clutched her #2 lead pencil, put on a brave face, and made her way to the adjunct city hall building. One glance at the test told her that she had over-studied. She had prepared herself for the "Steam-fitting Operator Level 1" position, not the lowly "Small Boiler Operator Level 3" which demanded only superficial knowledge of how steam worked, but much practical knowledge of filling and maintaining an actual furnace.

The test proved to be a 100-question multiple choice, easily accomplished. She clutched the document in its manila envelope as she waited for the Bus 15 to take her home.

"Look at this, Blue Jay!" she gloated, waving the certificate at him. "97 per cent! Lily Swan, Boiler Operator Extraordinaire! We're legal!"

"Congrats!"

"I only needed a 75 to pass! 97 per cent! If I fail out of grad school, I guess I can always become a steamfitter."

With this important step taken, Lily grew more comfortable with her position. Blue Jay reluctantly worked in some study time, and with Lily's expert coaching, managed to pass the test with a venerable 76. "Too bad they didn't just ask me to write an essay on "Three Reasons Why I want to become a Boiler Operator," he shrugged. "Or a poem: *Ode to the Great Fire-Breathing Dragon of Kewaunee.*"

The next time the temperature dropped into the thirties, they made a pilgrimage to the great Kewaunee boiler and gingerly turned on the intake water valve. Blue Jay stayed by the heavy metal boiler room door to make sure the Kewaunee clicked in, while Lily retreated to their apartment to turn up the thermostat.

"We have ignition, Houston!" Blue Jay shouted. "Blastoff!"

And the mighty boiler began to roar.

"On my next trip to the Goodwill, I'll have to buy a couple of frames and hang our licenses in the boiler room," Lily commented. "It's too bad they didn't put our scores on the certificates. 97%!" she gloated.

AROUND THAT TIME, to her surprise, Lily realized that she was making friends with some of the tenants. Some of them, such as Mrs. Grant and Mrs. Davis, had lived there forever, it seemed. Tannenbaum Arms was truly their home. Others, such as the students in the upper apartments, seemed to rotate in and out, with only some of the faces recognizable on a daily basis. This made Lily a bit edgy because legally the names of all tenants were to be registered with them and listed on the mailboxes. As she vacuumed the three flights of dusty carpet, she made up a television show, "Touring the Tannenbaum," similar in tone to *The Ed Sullivan Show*. She was, of course, the emcee, and rated the apartments and tenants.

The award for the most elegant apartment would have to go to Larry and Lenny, the two middle-aged men who had lived in

Apartment 1 for the past couple of years. On their first week here, Jay and Lily had been invited to tour their apartment. Lenny was an interior decorator and often received used items when re-decorating one of the elegant lakefront mansions a few blocks to the east. One of his finest coups was an Austrian crystal chandelier, which he and Larry had installed in the dining room at their own expense. They also had a stately leather couch studded with brass nails and—although neither of them played, as far as she knew—a baby grand piano ceremonially outfitted with a heavy silver candelabrum that Lenny said could have come from the Pabst mansion—beer baron friends of the original Tannenbaum family that had erected this apartment building in the 1920's, he noted.

Larry and Lenny gave a touch of class to the building, Lily thought, with their impeccable manners and style. They also always seemed to know what was going on in all the apartments. They were great conversationalists and generally shared all they knew about everyone, as if they were Lily's personal Tannenbaum news team. Lily wished they were home right then; she would have appreciated a kind word and an update.

Lily had been forewarned by Mrs. Grant to expect a terrible verbal brawl from Apartment 1 now and then, that once one had escalated to Lenny throwing some of Larry's personal effects out the window onto the lawn. Mrs. Grant further expounded, "I am not a gossip. I just want you to know so you won't be alarmed. We just act like nothing is wrong. It's just their way of coping. They're dear fellows. Every time I make banana bread, I take them some." Lily genuinely liked the Apartment 1 gentlemen. "So, Mrs. Grant *is* a bit of a gossip," she shrugged. She hadn't yet witnessed one of those rumored outbursts and thought perhaps Mrs. Grant had fantasized this. Whatever their personal anguish, she wished them the best. She would give them the top award for style and leave it at that.

Apartment 2. Mrs. Grant. What award for her? Perhaps loneliest. Or perhaps loveliest. Lily didn't know if Mrs. Grant was in her high seventies or low eighties. She appeared agelessly elderly. Her husband had died of influenza some time back, probably during the Depression, and she had raised their only daughter on a secretary's salary. Unless she had been a child bride, that would put her in her eighties. Now the daughter lived in California and came for rare visits perhaps once a year, according to Lenny. Mrs. Grant and Lily gradually were building a relationship of trust through the numerous favors Mrs. Grant had requested and Lily had politely accomplished—such as hauling out trash and unclogging the kitchen sink. She felt a grudging dislike for Mrs. Grant's daughter who could have made her mother so happy with a few more visits or even letters, who didn't seem to appreciate her. Mrs. Grant had her daughter's pictures displayed in every room.

"She's so different from my mother," Lily mused. When Lily was six her father had died of thyroid cancer, probably a result of chemical exposure during his service time in the Korean Conflict. She vaguely remembered him, mostly as a sleeping person on a day bed in the dining room with a blanket pulled over his head. After a year of weeping, her mother resolutely put the nightmare behind her, remarried when Lily was in second grade, and started a new life with a hard-working, hard-drinking biker. They created their little brown-eyed nuclear family of one boy and one girl, and Lily basically found herself the outsider—the ungainly, bookish swan child with her father's green eyes among the brown-eyed ducklings, best valued as a built-in babysitter. Although she had moved beyond bitterness, Lily still felt an occasional twinge of emptiness. Her mother hadn't even come from Tulsa for her marriage or the birth of her first grandchild, although both times she sent a Hallmark card and twenty dollars.

As the vacuum hummed, Mrs. Grant cracked open her door. “Oh, it’s you, Lily. Have you shopped yet today?’

Lily grinned, “No.” She fought a desire to say that she did not shop on a daily basis.

The sweet voice faltered. “I’m wondering if you could pick up a few things for me. I’d like a single lamb chop, Dearie. From the loin. Also, my cupboard door is stuck. I’m wondering if you could open it for me.” Although she appeared frail, Lily believed that Mrs. Grant was as tough as nails.

“I’ll knock on your door when I’m done vacuuming. If I stop now, I’ll never finish.”

Moving up the corridor, Lily speculated on what prize she might award to Mrs. Theresa Hopkinson, a staid business-woman in her early fifties, who lived alone in the spacious apartment. Lenny had informed her that it was an open secret that Theresa was in a private love relationship with a wealthy, twice-divorced banker whose current wife had developed a memory disorder, that she herself had married young and divorced young. However, because of the tenets of her faith, she would not re-marry. Every Sunday morning she went to eight o’clock mass at the nearby St. Peter and Paul’s; every Sunday around ten she came home with her small parcel of hard rolls and ham, which she purchased after mass at the Italian bakery on Brady Street. The all-knowing Lenny said Mrs. Hopkinson’s breakfast would be shared with the banker who seemed to arrive around eleven, often holding flowers as if they were the Holy Grail.

Larry and Lenny had told Lily about this, and she herself once had seen the genial gentleman caller ascend the stairs with a large bouquet of red roses. “Tenets or tendrils of faith? And to you, Mrs. Hopkinson, goes the award of Most Tasteful Tenant—for the discretion shown in your life and reflected in the quality of the traditional furnishings and beige walls of your domicile." And she hastened to add, "Or maybe the Most Wasteful Tenant—for throwing away all possibility of happiness." Lily caught herself here, realizing she was not always kind, prone to snap judgments based on hearsay. "Or maybe I just don't get it," she corrected herself. "Not every woman wants to balance a baby on her hip or smile across the table at a man every morning. Maybe this is her road to happiness."

The vacuum cleaner hummed on and Lily began humming with it—some kind of John Philip Sousa marching song that seemed an appropriate tempo for cleaning duty. She further speculated on happiness: perhaps Mrs. Hopkinson and the banker would have been truly miserable had they married, because she would have had to compromise her religious views and he would have been guilt-ridden about leaving his ailing wife. But it seemed to Lily that there should have been a way around this impasse. She would have to further discuss this with Lenny. "Don't become a petty busybody, Lily," she admonished herself.

Next came the entrance to Apartment 4, home of Mrs. Davis. "Let's see," thought Lily, remembering the episode when Mrs. Davis tried to accost her with her cane. "Most Warlike. Or let's be more positive. Hardiest. Strongest Survival Instinct." Except for a glimpse of a mouse gray carpet through a crack in the door, Lily had not seen the inside of this apartment. Lily had learned from Mrs. Grant that in keeping with her spirit of self-reliance, Mrs. Davis boasted that she had been to a doctor only once in her life, and that was over ten years ago already when she had a gall bladder attack shortly before she turned eighty. Careful not to bump the door with the vacuum cleaner, fearing Mrs. Davis would think she was knocking, Lily quickly proceeded up the final flight of stairs. Visions of the austere Grecian profile with gray hair in a severe bun spurred her on.

The third-floor tenants were the most elusive. Of course,

there was Moisette, who threw herself all over any man within sniffing distance. She had two roommates, Linda and Sarah. Unlike Moisette, they seemed like hard-working community college students, both waitressing at the nearby George Webb's and studying when they weren't in class, with very little time for partying. "What award should I give them?" mused Lily. "Most Scheduled? No, that would be me. Least Known? No, that would be the guys in Apartment 6. I'll settle for Most Tolerant, because they put up with Moisette as a roommate. She'd drive me crazy in half a day."

With only a scant three feet of carpet to go, the vacuum cleaner died. Lily realized that the extension cord didn't quite reach and had come unplugged. Through the door of Apartment 6 she heard Beatles music blasting on the stereo, sending a message that everybody should drop out. "Great," she thought. "I'm done. I'm dropping out. I might morph into a walrus if I stay here too long! I think I'll just skip the rest of the hall. Nobody will notice the difference. They're probably higher than the ceiling right now. All I am saying is *I am he as you are he as you are me and we are all together!*" she sang along. "And now this job is done."

Bumping the old vacuum tank down the stairs, the hose coiled around her shoulders, she proclaimed, "And now, ladies and gentlemen, the winner is...... Well, we'll just let everyone hang in suspense until next week's vacuuming be-in while the judges tabulate the score. So for now, goodbye and good luck from Lily Swan, charming hostess of your favorite Monday night show, *Tannenbaum Arms*. Now stay tuned for *I Love Lucy*."

As she was about to leave the building, Lily turned around and looked up the stairs, startled by a blood-curdling scream. She stood attentively like an ancient snake goddess, vacuum cleaner hose twined around her neck. Would further screams ensue? Registering the thump and squeak of a corridor door being opened, she decided it was safe to go upstairs again to check things out. "After all," she asserted, "I am the formidable caretaker."

At that point, Moisette and Linda came down the stairs. "We have a mouse in the pantry!"

Lily tried not to laugh. "What's its name? Mickey? What are you feeding it?"

"Really!" Moisette stiffened. "This is no joking matter!"

"I'll have to get a trap. I think I'll try to find one of those humane ones. I'll give Mr. Dreschler a call," Lily responded.

"You expect us to go back up there?" Moisette asserted.

Linda grabbed her arm, "C'mon, Moisette. We left the door open. Maybe it's run away by now."

"Maybe I should run away, too," Lily mused as they descended the freshly vacuumed stairs. "Blue Jay is getting ready to participate in the Resistance Read-in and here I am, dealing with screaming tenants and walruses and dust bunnies. You don't need to be a Weatherman to know which way the wind blows."

THE NEXT EVENING as tranquility had settled over the building after supper, Jay absently remarked that it was getting dark so early these days. Lily sighed and thought about throwing a load of diapers in the washer before attacking her homework. Suddenly the harsh ring of the doorbell assailed them. Jay jumped up from the kitchen chair where he had been lingering over coffee. "My turn," he said. Lenore began to howl in a disarmingly beagle-like way. The Hatchling started giggling and shaking his legs as if pedaling an invisible tricycle.

Mr. Dreschler stood in the doorway, a torn newsprint poster

in his hand. “I suppose you are responsible for this?” he accused.

“Whaa?”

He held out a crumpled poster of a frowning, uniformed police officer, badges flashing on jacket and cap—***Wanted for Crimes against the People: Sergeant Frank Miller, head of MPD’s Tactical Squad. We demand that Sgt. Miller be summarily dismissed from the MPD and brought to justice by the people.***

“Mrs. Grant and Mrs. Davis both called. This was hanging in the front hall over the mailboxes. You responsible for this?” He looked at Jay.

“No. And the ladies should have called me.”

“This could lose you your happy home, you know.” Mr. Dreschler looked around, first resting his eyes on the kitchen linoleum landscaped with graham crackers, then the sink heaped with dirty dishes. “This poster fits my definition of un-American propaganda! Maybe treason!”

He pointed at the words while reading them, as if Lily and Jay were illiterate. “Calls the tactical force of the police department ‘the Goon Squad’ and ‘Miller’s Marauders.’ Charged of ‘general inability to function as a feeling member of the human race.’ I know Chief Brier personally. He ordered the tactical squad to clamp down on rabble-rousers and drug users. Sgt. Miller is just doing his job.”

He paused and made jabs in the air with his index finger, pointing at Jay. “You need to be in charge here. This is a first-class operation. Keep order. Keep peace. I don’t need to lose my best tenants and you don’t look ready to move.”

“No, Sir!” Jay replied.

“We didn’t know. I will make it a point to check the front hall twice a day,” added Lily, trying to smooth things over. “Look. We can handle this.”

"I hope so," he replied. "These are some tough times to get through with all spoiled brat protestors from all over the country coming here to cause trouble calling themselves White Panthers and Black Panthers. It used to be simple. Just UWM Panthers on the basketball court."

Lily and Jay exchanged looks. "Sure. We'll do our best to keep things in line here in the building," Lily responded.

"Tough times all around," Jay added.

"I shouldn't have to be bothered with this nonsense." And with that, without even a simple goodnight, Mr. Dreschler let himself out.

Lily held up the ragged poster. "It's going on the fridge," she said. "My favorite line these days is 'Give Peace a Chance.'"

"No." Jay reached for the poster. "We don't need his mug in our kitchen."

Lily shrugged. "Choose your battles, married lady," she coached herself. "Okay, then."

JAY CONTEMPLATED TAKING on a work-study job as a security guard in the library on Tuesday and Thursday nights, against Lily's better judgment. Lily thought they should wait until the campus children's center could materialize so he could work while The Hatchling was in daycare. Jay reasoned that the library job was relatively non-demanding, and he could study just as well there; but after thinking it over he realized that it would soon be winter and the demands of the caretakership would increase. Also, The Hatchling was becoming more mobile and would soon need more energy expended into caring for him.

Word was around that a large protest march was for October 15, a Moratorium. Lily's entire class decided to boycott their Puritan Morality seminar scheduled for that night and join the marchers. At this point, Lily persuaded Jay that they should go. "The Hatchling will be safe on my back," she stated.

He agreed, on the condition that they could simply back off and pull away if there seemed to be too much rising tension. He recalled his Chicago experiences—the senseless brutality, the taunts exchanged on both sides, cries of "Fascist Pig!" and "Dirty Commie Hippies!" filling the streets; and in response, the relentless clubs coming down indiscriminately. "Even though it's UWM, not Chicago, things can flare up in seconds," he warned. "I want you to agree beforehand to trust my judgment on this."

She frowned, paused. Then smiled. "Agreed."

The march proved to be relatively balanced, even verging on peaceful at times, with only a handful of disorderly conduct citations. SDS members handed out black armbands. Officers were strategically placed along the route, but nobody seemed to be looking for trouble. The streets were so filled with protesters that there was no room even on the sidewalk, stretching from the university to downtown six miles away, moving like a wave. It seemed to be a rare time of coming together of the diverse student body that comprised UWM. People from groups ranging from the Yippies, to the White Panthers, to the Black Panthers, to the Vietnam Vets for Against the War, and every group in between decided to drop their own differences for a night and concentrate on making a unified statement about ending the war. Not only students participated, but people of all ages from the surrounding communities made their presence known. Along with indignation and distress over the political situation, there seemed to be an atmosphere of tolerance and gritty humor. President Nixon had talked about a silent majority that supported the U.S. war effort; as if in direct opposition, someone carried a sign reading "Silent Majority for Peace."

Two students who looked like they had come from the nearby public high school passed out cheese sandwiches. Signs with slogans such as "End the War Before it Ends You" and "Bring the Troops Home" were passed around. Someone handed Jay a sign that read "Draft Beer, Not Students." For a while, Lily carried "Make Love, Not War," but it proved too much with The Hatchling on her back, so she passed it on.

Hundreds of students marched from the Union, south on Downer Avenue, then over onto Prospect Avenue, lined with its high-rises and homes of former glory, now converted into apartments and rooming houses. John Lennon's spirit pervaded through his new protest song, anger absorbed into the beauty of the melodic plea: *All we are saying is give peace a chance.* Repeating the refrain over and over as they walked, the voices mingled and harmonized, echoing through the streets. *Everybody's talkin' 'bout evolution, revolution, devolution. All we are saying.....* Snug in his back carrier, The Hatchling fell asleep.

Jay and Lily were joined up with two of Jay's commando-booted buddies who had protested with him in Chicago, as well as several Birkenstock-clad members of Jay's "Poets for Peace" resistance group.

As they approached the War Memorial, some SDS members handed out candles from a wicker laundry basket and people held them high. By now, evening had fallen and the candles illuminated the darkness like flickering SOS signals all around. A platform and microphone appeared as if by prearranged magic, and anyone who wanted to take the stage could get up and give a speech.

Voices rose in protest of the war, with references to atrocities seen on television that gave immediacy and urgency to the scene. An impassioned veteran with a leg wound recalled an event of U.S. troops of Company C slaughtering a whole village full of people. This was news to everyone. Hearing his personal account, the crowd became increasingly agitated.

"End the War! Bring our Troops Home!" One person spoke wearing a skeleton suit that glowed in the dark. "I am death. How many more will join me in the grave before this is over? 45,000 of our troops already dead, half a million deployed. Richard Nixon, this is on your soul!"

Things grew more intense. The officers made their presence known, standing in defensive mode at the edges of the street like Spartan warriors. Lily and Jay decided to make their exit and began the long walk home.

"I can wear The Hatchling for a while," offered Jay; but Lily declined because she was afraid the transfer would wake him up.

They somberly walked through the streets, Lily pondered, "What kind of world will today's children have to grow up in? I think every generation tries to make it better. I hope we can succeed. But is it really a revolution or just a repetition?"

"Damn that war!" Jay exploded. "The world has a long way to go. What kind of times are these? I hope our voices are heard."

"Maybe we're making it better," Lily mused.

Jay reached over to the bulge in the back carrier and gave the sleeping Hatchling a pat. "Maybe. I hope so."

They walked on in silence.

October brought no peace. It ended with the ongoing trial of the Chicago 8, soon to become the Chicago 7 with the departure of Bobby Seale. Protestors were brought to trial, charged with crossing state lines and conspiring to incite a riot and other transgressions during the violent demonstrations at the Democratic National Convention the previous summer. Judge Julius

Hoffman seemed to delight in tangling with the defendants, especially Abby Hoffman who taunted him with, "Dad, Dad, have you forsaken me?"

"These contenders are made for each other," Lily remarked. "Opposites with big mouths and beliefs in righteous causes attract."

Daily reports filled the news.

Jay took more than a casual interest in the trial, since he had participated in the Chicago demonstrations in August. On October 29, things took a worse turn, when Black Panther Activist defendant Bobby Seale attempted to disrupt the trial. He continued to shout insults and make obscene and provocative comments at the judge and prosecuting attorney and even the onlookers. Judge Hoffman ordered Bobby Seale bound and gagged. This played out on national television, prompting passionate response on all sides.

'Repulsive! Abhorrent! The term 'kangaroo court' comes to mind. This would have made incredible, outrageous theater," Jay remarked at a conclave of the Poets for Peace as they met in the Union and watched the five-thirty news. "Except it is real. It is horrific. If we had written this, nobody would have believed it."

There were murmurs of agreement, as the next story flashing on the screen showed a recent bombing of a rice paddy in Vietnam, appearing deceptively innocent, although purportedly a Viet Cong stronghold.

"Words fail," remarked a tall poet named Sam.

"No. Words can't let us down. Poetry can be a form of protest, a voice of the people, a collective conscience," a woman with long braids countered. Jay knew them both from various English classes he had taken over the past three years. He nodded in agreement.

"So, do we look at words as weapons waging war for peace?" he chimed in.

Another member, Val, took the bait. "They can be, at times, but that is not their total function. As the great S.I. Hayakawa says, 'The symbol is not the thing it symbolizes and the word is not the thing.'"

"Hey, we all took that course, Val," another poet entered the arena. "I say we just speak out from a voice of authenticity. Best way to counter media propaganda."

"Time for an open reading again," Jay remarked, "even if we are only preaching to the choir."

The news ended with a cute story of heartwarming comic relief about a cat that was lost by people camping in Ohio that somehow ended up in Florida where its owners lived. The poets, hearts filled with deep unease that could not be assuaged by a cat story, went their separate ways.

CHAPTER 3
NOVEMBER

Wherein Mrs. Grant and Mrs. Davis launch their Civil War of Heat, Apartment 5 has a rodent infestation, Apartment 6 needs a plumbing repair, and Blue Jay is invited to read with the iconic poet, Gary Snyder

November in Milwaukee is a time to bring out the winter coats and crank up the heat. Lake Michigan keeps her humans air conditioned in the summer with her lake breezes, but once winter sets in, her cold, damp lake air chills to the bone. On one such bone-chilling afternoon, Blue Jay received a phone call from Peter Sterns, a friend from his writing class—a fellow poet who shared his sensibilities. "I have news, Jay! News too big for the phone! Come meet me over here at the Tux."

Bundling up the Hatchling in his bright turquoise snowsuit and plopping him into his back carrier, Blue Jay and the Hatchling promptly set forth, undaunted by the blustery wind. The bar smelled of cigarette smoke and stale beer, the music was blaring, but the tables near the window were perfect for watching shoppers pass by.

This small shopping area tucked among staid apartments and duplexes served the needs of an eclectic mix of students, up-and-coming professionals, and older people who had discovered the area a good forty or more years before. The closer one got to the lake, the more impressive the turn-of-the-century houses became, their Old World influence apparent in the Victorian turrets and gingerbread trim and the even older yellow brick Italianate homes with their carved stone lintels and brick quoins stationed at the corners like rigid bodyguards. Heading in the opposite direction, away from the lake and toward the Milwaukee River, the single-family residences were smaller, Arts-and-Crafts-style bungalows interspersed with frame duplexes and the occasional brick apartment building.

No matter which side of the divide the East Siders came from, everyone felt comfortable at The Tuxedo Bar on Downer. The usual afternoon bartender, Eddie Orvino, carried around his rolled-up manuscript of original song lyrics in his hip pocket, ready to share them at the slightest hint of eagerness from a patron. He nodded a greeting as Blue Jay entered. Eddie's appearance was—well, unique.... Blue Jay wasn't one to notice hair styles, but in this case he always secretly marveled at Eddie's famed jet-black pompadour. It looked stiff as a board, every hair as intact as if it were made of wire bristles. Once a drinking buddy had dared Jay to touch it to see if it was real, but he declined, not wanting Eddie to think he was making a pass.

Blue Jay scanned the room looking for Peter. Corner tables seemed to be reserved for serious writers; there was usually someone oblivious to the world filling a yellow legal pad with some creative endeavor. Nobody gave you the bum's rush at the Tux, or even insisted that you buy a drink. On Thursday evenings, out of courtesy the blasting music was lowered and a group of poets took over and held impromptu readings to an appreciative crowd of students and locals. Blue Jay often counted himself among them.

"Jay, my man!" a voice called from over by the pool table. Peter was the enthusiastic type, ready to fall into a rumbling laugh over the slightest peculiarity of human nature. He was a fellow poet, given over to recreating the archaic sonnet form with slant rhyme and dazzling imprecision. He often had the Tux crowd wowed into puzzled silence when he read. Jay always felt that Peter's poems were made to be deciphered slowly on paper, so as to catch the subtleties. However, Peter's booming voice gave the words an undercurrent of percussion that made up for a lack of understanding, and everyone loved his readings.

"What's your hot news? I've just walked five blocks wearing a baby on my back for you."

"I just heard it from Morgan Gibson! I wanted to let you in on the ground floor. Gary Snyder and Galway Kinnell are reading in Milwaukee, right here at UWM."

"What? By us?" Blue Jay sometimes showed signs of the widespread Midwestern Inferiority Complex, an ailment afflicting many who had received the societal message that one had to go to either the East or West Coast to be considered the Genuine Product. It was sort of okay to be *from* the Midwest, like Bob Dylan who had to change his name from Zimmerman and move to New York to get noticed; but to remain *in* the Midwest was almost to seal your literary or artistic doom. Gary Snyder was a man of the world, in Blue Jay's opinion. He had lived in Japan as a Buddhist monk—and in India and Indonesia, had worked on the docks in California, sailed on an oil tanker in the Pacific. Blue Jay knew several of his poems by heart. He couldn't help himself: "Wildness. It is perennially within us, dormant as a hard-shelled seed, awaiting the fire or flood that awakes it again."

"Enough already, Jay." Peter winced. "Yeah. Us. Here. He's coming for a Poetry Weekend, sponsored by our very own UWM English Department. He's going to read first and then we'll have cameo appearances by some of us local yokels. Wanna read?"

Blue Jay hesitated, "I think so. I don't know if I have anything good enough.

"Sure you do. Why don't you read your *Penitent Generals Walking on Tin Cans*?"

"Maybe I'll write something special for the occasion. Kinnell's cool, but...Gary Snyder! My type of poet! Far out!" Jay's voice trailed off as he contemplated meeting one of his favorite poets eye-to-eye. This idea would take some time getting used to. Snyder!

"You've got two weeks. He's coming middle of November. The 14th, I think."

"Enough time for several masterpieces. Let's talk more in depth on Thursday with the other poets. But now I'd better go. At this point, I think I'd better pick up a frozen pizza for our supper to appease the Kitchen Goddess. Thanks for the news to end all news!"

By the time Blue Jay and The Hatchling got back, Lily was waiting. "You could have at least left a note," she said. "I was worried. Not to mention, Lenore left a deposit in the doorway that I had to clean up."

"Oops! Sorry! You worry too much," he replied. "Look! Frozen pizza with sausage and mushrooms!"

They almost launched into one of their classic arguments that sprang up from this type of perceived misdeed, but when

Blue Jay told her about Gary Snyder's imminent visit, any possible slight was temporarily stored away (to be brought out later if necessary to fuel some future disagreement).

Jay and Lily rarely had arguments. Lily had learned at a young age to hide her emotions. Rather than express disagreement, she tended to withdraw, although increasingly she felt provoked enough to speak out. Jay, on the other hand, learned much earlier in the relationship when to back off or distract. Theirs was a peculiar partnership, a balance based on fairness and fondness.

This proved to be true two evenings after the Snyder/Kinnell announcement when Larry and Lenny came down for a visit. These visits were usually pleasant events involving lots of building news. This time, however, they offered Lily and Jay their 18-inch television set, still in good working order. They were replacing it with a state-of-the-art 27-inch set. Jay and Lily exchanged glances. "Thanks." Jay was about to decline, but he saw the look on Lily's face. "We have to think about it." The well-intentioned offer provoked a heated dispute well into the night.

Although television sets were common in most homes, Jay questioned a lifestyle that had developed featuring evenings huddled around the television set. A great development in the Upper Peninsula of his teen years had been the advent of TV trays—so people could actually eat supper watching television programs on the three available channels. When walking at night, he was appalled by houses darkened except for the blue-white flash and glow of the television screen. Their rooftop antennas perched like gigantic metal whooping cranes with nowhere to land, except when a sleet storm or some gale winds knocked them over. And sooner or later, it always happened, he thought.

"Absolutely not!" was Jay's initial response after the tenants had departed.

"Absolutely Yes!" responded Lily.

"We don't need it. I don't want it. We can catch enough news in the Union if we really need to see the bloodbath, and we have our radio. That's enough. And do we really want that kind of influence on Little Jay? Our son, the TV Zombie!"

"Well, actually, maybe not that extreme, but all things in moderation," Lily countered. "Not all television is bad. I caught a little bit of news about a new educational program in the student union yesterday. It's special for kids. Little kids. Called *Sesame Street*. It teaches them the alphabet with singing puppets."

Jay hesitated. "But what is the psychological effect of television viewing on the mind of a child? You're the sosh major. You should know that. The bad outweighs the good, in my opinion. I say no!"

"Well, I have some say here, too. Actually, 50%. That's our bargain, remember? It's simply puppets and music! How can that be so bad? And I would like a television. I'd like to watch the news, too. We watched the moon landing last summer. Did that warp you? This war is on screen, on the news. Don't you wanna know what's going on? Not around Little Jay, of course, but maybe catch the 10 o'clock news after he's asleep. What's wrong with that? You watch the news at UWM. This is the era of immediacy through the television screen. I don't want to be left out."

Jay scowled, as only he could, with his lower lip hardening into a straight line.

"Jay, let's get it on the basis of my wanting news programming, my call on this. Fair is fair. And we can watch this new Sesame Street program together a few times and decide later.

After all, he's only going on five months old, anyway. Plenty of time to think it through."

"I already sing him the ABC song. He doesn't need a puppet to teach him that," was Jay's last word.

In the end, a reluctant compromise was reached and the television was granted a spot in a corner of the living room the next afternoon.

ONE THING for sure about November weather in Wisconsin is its unpredictability. One day it's early winter, with flurries and looming cumulus cloudbanks. The next day there's a gentle reprieve, as if Indian Summer is struggling to stay. The heavens miraculously beam with eye-hurt bright blue and otherwise-stalwart citizens are tempted to steal away from jobs and schools to soak up one last bit of balm before winter truly settles in. On such a day, Mrs. Grant and Mrs. Davis launched their Civil War.

There was a definite chill in the air and Lily realized that even wearing her heavy sweater, she was shivering. Just then the telephone rang. It was Mrs. Grant: "What's the story on the heat? It's as cold as a barn!"

"Hi, Gramma Grant." (By now they were on familiar terms.) "I know. I'm freezing, too, even though it's nice and sunny. I'll turn on the heat. Stand by for steam."

A quick peek at the boiler's water gauge assured her that everything was ready. She turned up the thermostat and settled down with a sociology text, The Hatchling crawling around on the floor with Lenore and his plastic stacking donuts.

Twenty minutes later, they were surrounded by cozy warmth, the radiators pleasantly whispering like so many rustling reeds. "Do you know what they're saying, Baby Jay? They're saying, 'King Midas has donkey's ears!'" Lily often reverted to mythological allusions when she was in a mellow mood. She thought it gave a little grandeur to their daily duties; besides, it made her laugh.

Just then the phone rang. It was Mrs. Davis: "What are you trying to do? Kill us all? Turn that heat off immediately!"

Lily was beginning to regret that they had chosen to have their phone placed in the kitchen, directly outside the nursery. The ringing always was harsh and insistent. "Well, some of the tenants were cold and wanted to warm up. I won't leave it on all day or anything. We'll just take the chill off."

"By rights I should report you to Mr. Dreschler for squandering building funds. Fuel oil is expensive. This is why we keep getting our rents raised."

"It'll be taken care of," Lily said, biting her tongue to keep from saying something equally sassy.

Although Lily didn't know it at the time, this was only the first skirmish in a long winter's war. As she hung up the receiver, she marched into the hall and turned down the thermostat, all the while singing "The Battle Hymn of the Republic." The Hatchling set down his plastic donut and stared. The peculiar pitch of her singing must have struck a nerve with Lenore who lifted her head and began to moan.

As November 14, the day of the great Snyder reading drew closer, spirits rose among the English majors on campus. Professors Barbara and Morgan Gibson encouraged all their students to attend, even those who were taking their courses for an "easy three credits." The momentum grew, becoming a real campus event as SDS and Poets for Peace, along with assorted Yippies and Panthers, both Black and White, took up the cause. "It is the age of poetry!" Jay mused. "Poetry can be power. Something good is coming out of the mess. Maybe..."

Besides the activists, there was the mass of regular students who agreed in principle with much of the protests, but who were not inclined to actively participate in boisterous shows of opposition. Many held part-time jobs and their educations were on the line. For others, it was necessary to keep a good academic record so they could evade the draft.

Then on November 12, word of the My Lai Massacre began to spread on campus. Students convened in the union and stared in silence as the news unfolded. The slaughter had happened the previous March, but the huge cover-up finally had broken. The horrors of My Lai flared anew in the group consciousness. More details hit the news. Captain Ernest Medina had told the troops to destroy everything in that "Pinkville" that was "walking, crawling, or growing." The next morning Charlie Company C had moved relentlessly through the village, murdering men, women, children, and infants. Many victims were gang-raped and mutilated. Lieutenant William Calley, Jr., platoon leader, would now stand before a jury and be held accountable.

Lily and Jay, along with others, felt devastated. The frustration and anger on campus rose to intolerable levels. "Today felt like a time bomb waiting to explode," observed Jay over a shared lunch before Lily ran off to her classes. "Innocent villagers just like us, going about their lives. Women and children. Killed. Now we find out. Everybody is wound up tight as a drum. I ran into this dude I met a couple months ago, Krazy Wayne, he calls himself. He's not a student, but he hangs out on campus with the Vietnam Vets Against the War. He's saying he understands what went on. People go crazy over there. You live in fear. You can't tell your friend from an enemy ready to reach out for your hand with a grenade."

"I'd hate to be in ROTC right now," Lily observed. "Bolton Hall is going to be a little tumultuous this afternoon."

"Go ahead. Go to class. Just know when to duck and cover,"

Jay advised. "Smoke bombs or tear gas, stay close to the floor, and don't panic."

At that point, the Hatchling banged on his highchair and threw his spoon on the floor. Lenore got up from her special doggie rug and trotted over in search of a snack, causing the Hatchling to bang on his tray again, letting out a deep chuckle.

"Look who wants attention," Lily smiled. She stooped to pick up the spoon and stuck it into his hand, clasping his fingers around it. "Yum-yum! Carrots!" As she guided the spoon to his mouth she saw a glint of white. "Jay! Look! He has a tooth poking through! His third one! A little fang on the top!" At least for a few moments, mundane wonder of the third tooth blunted the dreadful news from Vietnam.

Distracted by the horrible news of My Lai coming at the same time as the imminent visit of the great poets Gary Snyder and Galway Kinnell, Blue Jay put aside his ambitious verse epic, *The Tragedie of Joanie Fist*, to create a work that would speak from his heart. At that moment, the epic seemed too ethereal, more an intellectual exercise than writing from the gut. He often ran his poems past Lily, but her comments weren't much help because she seemed to be a very uncritical audience. "Of course I love your work, because I love you," she'd say.

During November, Jay wrote at least a dozen poems, but none of them seemed right. He decided he needed to confer with his friend Peter in a meeting at the Tux that evening. Peter had decided to go for a religious deferment from the draft, taking a non-denominational Church of God correspondence class to enhance his clerical credibility. That night Peter appeared in a monk's robe.

"Ah, Brother Peter it is now, I guess. Can I read something to you? I need your honest, unbiased response."

"Well, sure. I only look this way for the narcs. Beauty is only skin deep."

Jay took a deep breath and began:

No Dove.
Dove Day is Over:
Peace! Oh, Peace!
I'm calling you!
Arrive noisily now
like a greedy robin
Welcome as spring
Digging for glowing treasure in the grass---
A peace worm!
(Too many souls have gone to grievous anonymity
Leaving their dear ones here,
To deal with empty beds and hollow songs;
Reach up to the sweet peach tree of life,
Pluck a piece of peace.)
A peace peach!

Peace! Oh, Peace!
Arrive stridently!
I'm calling you!
Arrive roaring like a marching lion,
No more drafting or dodging;
No more ruthless offensives
In thatch-roofed villages and college campuses;
Use your angry voice
Demanding
Threatening.
Come striding,
Mane and hackles bristling,
Roaring and glistening.

Down bloodied paths.
The angry voice thunders true.

Or, if you choose:
Arrive miraculously, bouncing like a zealous puppy,
Yipping, drooling, wagging
Bounding into the arms of happy-faced children
Lapping, laughing.
A Peace Pooch!

Peace! Here, Peace!
Peace!

"RIGHT ON, Bro, I'd have to say it's heartfelt." Peter nodded his approval. "I think you might go with that one. But I still like *The Penitent Generals.*"

Jay laughed. "I'm still working on the end. I'm not sure."

Eddie the evening bartender came over. "I couldn't help but hear you. *The Penitent Genitals*! Awesome. That sounds hot! Why don't you come by Thursday and read that poem here, just as a warm-up, of course."

Blue Jay beamed. "Well, that's a poem I still need to work on. Sounds stimulating. I just might unless I come up with something better between now and then."

"Bless you, my son," Brother Peter chirped, lifting his glass.

~

On the day of the double reading, Gary Snyder read at 2:30, followed by the members of the Poets for Peace, and eventually followed by the evening reading of Galway Kinnell. The UWM poets would have two opportunities to read, following the bards. Snyder's reading went well, but Jay was a little too edgy about his imminent part in the afternoon to give it his full attention. Peter came in late and found a seat beside him. Their group filled the entire front row. Brother Peter read first—a moving "Blessings to the Draft Card Burners of Amerika." After he read, he pulled out a cigarette lighter and a scrap of paper and burned his draft card in effigy. The crowd broke out in whistles and claps.

Jay looked over the audience until he caught the sight of Lily in her red beret with The Little Hatchling Jay on her lap playing with his mother's love beads. Lily had discreetly chosen a seat near the exit in case the toddler decided to throw ruckus and they had to make a quick getaway. "My son's first poetry reading," Jay beamed. "It's a little crazy here."

Frank Baranski was the next reader. "Brother Peter is a hard act to follow, and I didn't bring my poem *Ode to my Draft Card* along." He looked out over the audience. "Well, this will have to do." He hesitated, took a deep breath, and began chanting his "Black Man on the Bridge" poem. His soft, urgent, persistent voice cut through the crowd and they listened in hushed silence, then broke into spontaneous applause.

"Frank is a master already," Blue Jay murmured to Peter seated on his left. "Quiet power ready to erupt. Dude has control."

Blue Jay was the third Poet for Peace reader. He looked out at the audience in the auditorium and found Lily, smiling at him reassuringly, with The Hatchling bright-eyed on her lap. He took a breath began: "I dedicate this poem to my son, and to all the other children who have been born in this time of war. May they find a peaceful world one day. May our words and actions help create this world." He paused, then began: "No Dove. Dove day is over...."

Following the successful reading, Blue Jay's writing workshop members had the opportunity to meet with Gary Snyder. They gathered around a battered table in the English Department office, listening intently as Snyder shared tales of times he spent with Allen Ginsberg and Jack Kerouac. Snyder proved to be a good communicator--open faced, serene, with a thatch of hair that fell over his right eye. He spoke about the importance of nature, the importance of devoting time to going inward into one's soul, even in times that demanded outward response. In a way, Jay thought, he reminded him of pictures he had seen of another great American poet, Carl Sandburg. The very presence of this poet strengthened his resolve. "I will stand in this tradition," he told himself.

Jay conjured up a favorite grove of pine trees by Lake Superior where he had retreated with his poetry notebook when he was in high school. "This is what I am meant to do. I realize that poetry does not exist in a vacuum, that words have impact and import, that this deeply ruptured world is the grist of true poetry."

As he looked about him, Jay felt relieved to have this temporary retreat into a cozy room of trust and good fellowship. The Poets for Peace breathed deeply and laughed at sly puns and corny jokes.

The group planned to meet at 5:00 for a communal supper at the nearby organic restaurant, Fertile Dirt, then attend the much-anticipated evening poetry reading with Galway Kinnell. Jay knew he had apartment and family obligations before the evening's grand finale, so he bade farewell and took a contemplative walk back to the English Basement.

Promptly, as if on cue, at 4:30 the telephone rang. It was

Mel in Apartment 6 to report that caretaker assistance was needed there immediately for a plumbing emergency.

~

"So, what's wrong with your pipes?" Blue Jay couldn't keep the edge off his voice.

"Well, the water in the sink won't drain out."

He sighed, glancing down at his tie-dyed shirt and new blue jeans. "I'm just ready to leave for an important meeting, but I'll be right up to check on it first." He set the receiver down with a thunk, visions of lost poetic experiences floating behind his eyes.

"Lily!" he called. "Guess what?"

"I heard," she replied. "Let's all go up and take a look. I'll put The Hatchling in his carrier." She laughed. "Both of us know enough about plumbing to fix a clog if it's caused by a hairball. Let's hope."

They clomped up the rear fire escape as the hands on the clock continued to circle.

When they surveyed the situation, it didn't take long to discover that this was not your ordinary plumbing problem. The kitchen had a strange acrid, paraffin odor clinging to it. On the table were at least a dozen half-pint milk cartons holding wicks embedded in wax.

"Candle making?" Lily queried.

Mel shrugged. He looked tired, a bit irked, too. "Well, sort of. It wasn't me, though. Craig and Jan thought they could sell them at the Holiday Craft Market at the Union next week."

"Does this relate to the clog?" Blue Jay jumped into the

conversation. He turned on the water, and the sink showed no sign of emptying.

"Don't ask me. I'm only the bearer of bad news, Dude," Mel shot back. "I just wanted to wash enough dishes to have supper." He gestured at the drainboard stacked with several days' meal remains.

Lily stuck her finger down the drain. It hit solid wax. "A snake won't work for this and neither will the usual drain opener," she said. "Did they really think they could dump hot wax down into the sewer?"

Mel gave a sheepish ogle. "Well, maybe...."

"Bargain with us on this," Lily said, looking first at Blue Jay and then at Mel. "You can wash a few plates for yourself in the bathroom tonight. Tomorrow we'll come up and take care of this. We put it off for tomorrow and we won't report it to Mr. Dreschler."

Blue Jay nodded. "We'll have to remove the pipe and heat it, I guess, to get the wax out. It'll be quite a job. I'll have to get a friend over who has some wrenches."

"Agreed."

BLUE JAY hastily grabbed his poetry notebook, kissed Lily and The Hatchling goodbye, and took off on foot for campus.

The plan was for Lily to put The Hatchling to bed and Linda from Apartment 5 had agreed to come down and babysit. It was the first time they were leaving their son without one of them in all his five months. "But he'll never know! He'll be asleep!" Blue Jay reasoned. "Of course, you shouldn't have to miss this, Lily. Snyder and the Poets for Peace is a once-in-a-lifetime event."

. . .

All went almost as planned. The toddler fell asleep, the plumbing event was deferred, and Lily found her place next to Blue Jay at the poetry reading. The poet of the night was Gallway Kinnell. Englemann Auditorium was again packed. Lily looked around at the adoring audience, surprised to see people of all ages. "Who said, 'Never trust anybody over 30?' That would be about half the crowd."

"The ageless beauty of the spoken word...." Jay countered.

Several of their friends expressed their anticipation, speaking to their neighbors in hushed tones, bedecked in India-print skirts and beads and braids. Lily had changed into her prized Guatemalan serape, which she wore over a black turtleneck sweater. It was easy to feel beautiful tonight. She sat back as the melodious voice of the poet filled the auditorium. Blue Jay sat upright, leaning forward, as if taking a visual that would last forever. "Eeeennnnnnnd the waaaaar."

Poem followed poem, mingling nature and protest. Halfway through the night, several people began chanting and dancing around the outer aisles. Apparently sensing the mood of the crowd, Kinnell began extemporizing a long, atonal, anti-war dirge. Jay and Lily exchanged glances, both sensing that this was a once-in-a-lifetime experience, and they were there. They held hands and got up to join the dancers.

The only downside of the night, if it could be called that, was that Kinnell ran long and the Milwaukee Poets for Peace were not given an opportunity to read for the evening crowd; they had to discreetly tuck away their humble offerings, perhaps to be read at a later date over at the Tux. "Who knows?" Jay consoled himself. "I just might write that *Penitent Genitals* poem and dedicate it to Eddie the Bartender in exchange for a free beer."

The following week led up to Thanksgiving. Everyone seemed weary, ready for a break. It dawned on Lily that they might want a typical feast this year, and that she would have to get a roaster pan. She had never made a turkey dinner but thought it couldn't be too hard if one had the proper equipment. Time for a trip to the St. Vinnie Thrift Shop; so the Saturday before the break, she and little Jay boarded Bus 22 and headed west. Blue Jay begged off, seeing this as a perfect block of time to resume work on his play. Lily loved the bumpy bus ride into the heart of the city, with its storefronts and laundromats and mom-and-pop restaurants. There were inevitably boys on bikes and people with dogs and babies hustling about. Today there was a nip in the air, so the relaxed feel of summer was replaced with a sense of urgency.

The bus stopped on North Avenue, a block away from the St. Vincent, the hulking Cream City brick building that housed three floors of treasure. She hoisted the child still in his back carrier, from the adjacent bus seat unto her back—a much-practiced move. The St. Vincent once had been a soft, pale yellow, but over nearly half a century had aged to a grimy gray. "Look at the treasure house, Hatchling Babe! I think we will have to find you a surprise here, too." She noticed that he was growing out of his sleepers and thought that they might add that to their shopping list.

A black, speckled enamel roasting pan was located for only a dollar, a bargain to be sure. Lily smiled, picturing it nestling a small turkey, perfectly browned, with stuffing oozing out. She had never made stuffing before but didn't think it would be overly hard to follow the directions on the bag of cubed bread she already had bought.

Moving on, she was tempted by some china-painted porcelain teacups from another century priced at only twenty-five cents each. She picked out four of them. As for the sleepers, there was nothing that looked right; although she found some striped t-shirts in 10-month size, so the Hatchling could grow into them by Spring. Then, near the front door as they were ready to leave, a treasure! A stroller! Lily pounced! It was a plaid wonder, with a little surrey-fringed top and an adjustable seat. The five-dollar price seemed a bargain, but pushed Lily's finances to the upper limit, leaving her just enough cash for the bus trip home. "This is too good to pass up!" she confided. "I don't always wanna wear you on my back. Wouldn't you like a nice stroller ride sometimes?" Even if he could have comprehended, he would not have replied; for he was curled up in his carrier, sound asleep.

THANKSGIVING WAS to be a quiet affair, and turned out as anticipated, with a stuffed turkey roasting in its pan, sweet potatoes, and green beans. Although the plates were mismatched, the porcelain teacups gave a festive air. For dessert Jay surprised them with a pumpkin pie from the nearby Sentry. The sky was filled with a few flurries, but not enough to start them shoveling. They planned to do building maintenance while the turkey baked, and then take a walk with Little Jay in his new stroller and Lenore on her leash; then spend the evening with various school assignments. Neighboring caretakers Ernie and Klara Warner left a plate of ginger cookies at their door. "We should be the ones sending over cookies to them," Lily remarked. "If they hadn't gone out on a limb for us over the boiler license issue, we wouldn't be living here...."

"...in the very lap of luxury," Jay added.

For an instant, the image of her mother pulling a batch of chocolate chip cookies from the oven flashed across Lily's thoughts. "Long ago and far away, but I hope everything is going okay with her."

"Maybe one of these days I'll get a cookbook at the Renaissance Book Shop or St. Vinnie's and try to bake something for them. Maybe chocolate chip cookies."

"Okay by me," Jay laughed. "I could be the cookie tester. Make sure they aren't poisoned. You can't give the whole batch away."

Action in the building was subdued, with most of the younger tenants home for the long weekend. Mrs. Davis entertained some Christian Science church ladies; Larry and Lennie were nowhere to be seen, probably sharing an elegant catered feast somewhere; Lily had invited Mrs. Grant to join them in the basement for the meal. She graciously declined but took the offer of having a plate brought up to her. For the time being, the civil war between Grant and Lee was in truce mode; although Lily observed that Mrs. Grant was wearing both a sweater and a jacket.

Deep into the evening, baby asleep, dog walked, dishes done, water level in the boiler checked, Lily and Blue Jay snuggled side by side on the wicker couch watching the ten o'clock news. His arm went around Lily as he pulled her closer. She let her head drop onto his shoulder. "In spite of the mess the world is in, we had an okay day here in Tannenbaum Arms," she said.

"Better than okay. Almost perfect," he mumbled, holding her in a deep embrace.

CHAPTER 4

DECEMBER

Wherein the Youth of the Nation Tremble over the Draft Lottery, more injustices occur in Chicago and the world, Lily Swan and Little Jay buy a bird; and Lily and Jay write several papers, throw a holiday soiree, and welcome in Baby New Year

THE FIRST DAY of December was chill, with a dusting of frost but no snow, with overhanging gray clouds scurrying towards the lake. It was the kind of weather that the Lost Lenore loved to prance about in, and she was eager for her early morning walk. She nudged Jay from slumber, her wet nose pushing on his arm. "Wake up, Master! Get your fur on. Where's my leash? Let's get going!"

Jay groaned and reached out to scratch her ears. "Is it that time already?" He had studied for a German test until after midnight. Now he felt that he really wanted to stay under those covers another hour.

Lily nudged him. "Your turn to walk her and she knows it.

Just be quiet so you don't wake The Hatchling." She rolled over and put her pillow over her eyes.

"Eins, Zwei, Drei. Say Good Bye. Two, Three. Poor me. Two, Three, Four. Out the door." And he was up, grabbing for his jeans.

As he and Lenore were leaving, his relatively good mood instantly soured. He remembered that it was December 1, the day of the Selective Service Lottery. Now he was fully awake, confronting the future.

There had been a lot of muttering about this on campus. There had not been a lottery since World War II in 1942, but President Nixon and his cronies thought it might help their image and create more of an illusion of fairness, since so many people from inner cities and rural areas were getting drafted, while middle class boys schemed to dodge the draft legally or became perpetual students or had helpful family connections. Under the present system, the "oldest" young men who couldn't get deferments, or chose not to, were drafted first, starting with age 26 and working down. Jay knew he could be called if he lost his academic deferment and hoped that his chances might improve through the new lottery.

Jay realized the inequities. Academic deferments were helpful, but not everybody could be a college student—or wanted to be one, for that matter; but the thought of going to a jungle to fight in a war that seemed senseless and unjust, then maybe coming home in a body bag motivated plenty of students to stay in school as long as they could. He had heard that 130 young men had been killed in action just in the last two weeks of November

Jay also knew some people who claimed to be homosexual or encumbered with "bad backs." Someone even intentionally broke his arm in a door to become ineligible. Often family doctors were happy to oblige with health statements. One crony went to the draft board in full Nazi regalia pretending to be a Neo-Nazi spouting racist slogans and was immediately rejected. He proudly boasted of this creative performance. And. of course, some took the religious route like the pious poet, Brother Peter.

"Selective Service," thought Jay. "Chosen. Final Selection. Special Invitation for Servanthood. Dictating our future." As Lenore tugged on her leash at the sight of a poodle down the street, Jay tugged back and resumed his line of thought. He recalled hearing about an incident a few weeks earlier.

The head of the Selective Service, Lieutenant General Louis Hershey, top dog in charge of the draft, had been in Madison. Wherever the old general went, there were bound to be protests. In Madison his car had been egged. Jay recalled hearing that a man followed him around and mocked him, wearing a "General Hersheybar" costume with all kinds of medals on his chest and a toy fighter jet dangling from his side. Jay had shrugged when he heard this. "What good would this do?" he questioned. "But, then, what good can another antiwar poem do? We all bear witness to history in our own way, I guess."

The new lottery deal was supposed to end this hostility and institute a certain fairness back into who would be called. Everyone between 18 and 26 would be on equal footing, called to service solely by date of birth.

Instead, the mere thought of it already rattled the students. Jay felt relatively secure in his status as a student, at least for the time being until his graduation in June; but many of his friends were at risk. The drawing would be televised that night, and they were meeting at The Tux to watch the show on a large 27-inch screen.

His inner ditty continued, twisted and churned: "Eins, Zwei. We'll get by. Drei, Vier . Have no fear!"

He sighed.

"Or Drei, Vier. Have a beer. No, too early in the morning for that."

It would, after all, be a long day. Lenore spotted the red bricks of Tannenbaum Arms and tugged on her leash, pulling him back to the moment at hand.

THE AFTERNOONS WERE SHORTENING; soon it would be the time of the winter solstice. It was gloomy by 4:30 when Lily got home and put a frozen pizza in the oven, doctored with fresh mushrooms and onions. Val and Bob from the Poets for Peace stopped by and were urged to share supper.

Bob had recently joined a transcendental meditation group and was thinking how to incorporate his newfound outlook into his poetry. "I really dig Maharashi Mashesh Yogi. My girlfriend told me about him and I joined this group that she was already in."

Lily was curious to learn more. She had seen a group chanting in the mall by the union. "And... what does this do for you?"

"It brings us together and our hearts beat as one. Same overall guru as the Beatles, but we have a local guru Sri Siddharta who has been trained by the Maharishi. He has given me a mantra. We all get mantras. Well, I can't tell you what it is. It's private. Pure sex. Has a meaning in Hindu. This has a great calming effect and I think if everybody did this, we could attain world peace."

"Well, it sounds a hell of a lot better than what's happening in Nam. Maybe Uncle Sam needs a secret word," Val opined.

"You all could join if you want," Bob offered. He looked around. "This kitchen is a perfect spot for meditation." He eyed the steam pipes running across the ceiling. "Some meditators claim to have out-of-the-body experiences. Floating above the whole world, looking down." He smiled at Lily. "You might give it a try."

Lily laughed, "Why do you say that?"

"You look a little stressed. The dreamy cream color on these kitchen walls! Ethereal, and yet in a basement!"

Lily and Jay watched their pizza disappear. Lily privately thought that perhaps if their guests weren't wolfing down all the pizza so quickly, she might not be so stressed.

"Jay, you should eat faster," Lily nudged him.

After grabbing the last remaining slice of pizza, Val reached into his jacket pocket and brought out three chocolate bars. "I was saving these for the Tux, but let's eat these for dessert now in honor of Old General Hersheybar," he said, breaking them into their little squares and even placing a piece on the Hatchling's high chair tray as he spoke. Jay and Lily exchanged glances.

"Why not?"

The Hatchling picked it up and looked at it curiously, then shoved it into his mouth. A moment later, his face broke into a slobbery smile, chocolate running from the corners of his mouth. He had just experienced his first taste of chocolate.

"The Hatchling and I are happy to sit this one out," Lily said as the men were leaving. "Good luck to all of you. I expect a full report." She tried to appear calm but couldn't keep the edginess out of her voice.

It was a meditative walk through the darkening night. In the bar, the tables were pushed back against the walls to make room for extra seating. The 27-inch black-and-white television had been moved to the corner of the bar. People, mostly youthful males, were somber, hunched over their beers in spiritless conversation. Usually there was music blasting, but not tonight, Eddie the Bartender tried to create a more relaxed atmosphere by cracking a few bad jokes, but that only served to heighten the tension. Nobody really wanted to know why the chicken crossed the road this time.

"To get to Canada?" quipped a voice from a nearby barstool.

Precisely at 7 PM, the somber baritone voice of CBS commentator Roger Mudd sounded through the waves and the commencement of the drawing was viewed nation-wide.

"Thousands of people are huddling around their television sets all over the country tonight," Jay thought. His II-S Student Deferment was good for a few months, yet, then might become meaningless. "This is really the luck of the draw. Grad school might not be such a bad option if I can get accepted, but competition is stiff. Maybe we need a grad school lottery, too."

He looked around at the faces of friends and strangers gathered at the Tux. He understood that futures of thousands of young men between ages 18 to 26 all around the nation, were contained in those plastic capsules the size of Easter eggs, each harboring one of 366 numbers. First there was an invocation; then the drawings began:

NUMBER 258. That is September 14, the two hundred fifty-eighth day of the year. Assigned Lottery number 001. All young men born on this date between 1944 and 1950 would be first drafted.

NUMBER 114. April 24. 002.

"Second in line. Called up, for sure." Comments and barbs flew with each call. "I love my country, but this is just wrong!"

‘"I love my country. My country right or wrong."

"Wrong!"

Somebody let out a loud moan.

"I hope you get a low number."

"Fuck you!"

NUMBER 364. December 30. 003.

"Start celebrating early and then party hard this New Year's Eve."

A woman Jay did not recognize burst into tears and clutched the dark-haired man next to her. And so the hour progressed. Numbers were met with whistles of relief and hisses of disbelief. "Where did they find those students to do the dirty work of drawing the numbers?" someone questioned, noticing the procession of dutiful youths chosen to draw the numbers.

Occasionally the crowd responded in anger or sympathy as someone acknowledged a date. Jay's friend Val had been born on Valentine's Day, not too happy to be 004. "Old enough to fight, but not old enough to vote. Canada's looking better every day," he shrugged. "I need a plan." He paused. "No, Jay. That's not how we operate in my family. I'll go. I could never face my dad if I didn't."

After the first 30 numbers were called, Jay began to relax. He had heard that was the projected number to expect to be drafted this year. Eventually he learned he was number 247, June 22. The luck of his birth had given him a reprieve, at least for this year. "The undeclared war already has gone on for five years, over 40,000 soldiers are killed. For what?" he thought. Jay knew a night of serious deliberation with friends lay ahead. He gave Val a light punch on the shoulder. "Let's go find Bob."

"A free drink of your choice to anyone in the first 100!" Eddie called out. "I-A is a terrible place to be. Glad I'm an old man of 53!"

"Bad joke," someone called out.

"Anybody have a Quaalude? I need something stronger than beer," a surly man in a camo jacket muttered.

No one wanted to go home.

It was the kind of night that called for camaraderie and commiseration.

. . .

Three days later, more bad news broke. The Black Panthers Party in Chicago had a rising star, Fred Hampton. He and friend Mark Clark were asleep in their Chicago apartment, Fred in bed with his girlfriend, when heavily armed police barged in the front and back doors—eight in the front and six in the back.

It was a surprise raid. They fired over 90 shots, dragging Fred's pregnant girlfriend from his bed and shooting him repeatedly.

The next morning, pictures of the blood-stained mattress and bullet-hole-ridden walls were on television. Jay did not hear this news until he was at Bolton Hall and took a flyer from the local Black Panthers group that had quickly assembled in protest.

Jay felt sickened by the never-ending stream of events that seemed to be relentlessly unfolding. This one seemed particularly egregious. "We might never know the whole story," he ventured. He went through his class mechanically, listening to the conversations around him, but not feeling in a talkative mood. Instead of taking notes on a lecture on Goethe, he began a poem:

Eight marauders at the Front Door,
Six at the Back,
Pounce on
Nine sleeping Panthers
Clad in Black.
Ninety-nine bullets
Slamming through the night.
Seven minutes later:
No one left to fight.
Mark. Slain in the dark.
Fred. Dead.

In his bed.
And
Now
I
Let my silent rage bleed all over this page.

THE HOUR DRAGGED ON. The professor droned on. Usually Jay loved to think about Faustian bargains with the devil and the finer points of the soul's incomprehensible depths, but today he couldn't wait for the class to end.

ON THE MORNING of the first snowfall deep enough to track a cat, Lily arose in a festive mood. "O, Tannenbaum!" she sang, dancing around the kitchen table with The Hatchling in her arms. Since they were in an English basement apartment, the snow drifted snugly halfway up the windows, giving Lily the impression that they were in an igloo. "Let's have a party!" she suggested.

Blue Jay sat at the kitchen table staring at the puffy marshmallow melting in his mug of hot chocolate. "Yeah. Along with writing a term paper, studying for exams, and finishing *The Tragedie of Joanie Fist* over the break. Oh, yeah. Sell my soul. Shovel snow. Give blood."

Lily leaned over him and took a sip from his mug. "So what? Stop worrying. We don't need much this year and The Hatchling's too little to know the difference. I think I'll make him a set of finger puppets. He's almost big enough not to eat them."

"This snow is nothing compared to Yooper snow. You could shovel this Milwaukee snow with a pancake spatula."

Lily paused, intuiting that the issue not being discussed had to do with his parents and his sister Violet and not visiting them over the break.

Jay hesitated. "When I was a teenager, I couldn't wait to get away from home. The isolation I felt inside me seemed to be the same as the isolation surrounding me." He paused, "But now I don't know...."

The sentence hung between them, unfinished.

Divergent lifestyles had created a distance greater than the 220-mile trip to Northern Michigan. Jay's parents ran a ma-and-pa restaurant in Marquette, Michigan—Joe's Do Drop Inn—and always had to mind the shop; the restaurant business had faltered but staggered on when the iron mines closed, and Blue Jay and his sister Violet had secretly re-named it the Few Drop Inn, except when Blue Jay was having one of his moments and called it the Don't Drop Inn; or when really in a foul mood, Do Drop Dead.

The siblings knew that the tasty hamburgers fried up and smothered in onions were often made from venison illegally purchased at the restaurant's back door from Ottawa Indians who did not feel bound by the hunting restrictions imposed upon them by the Department of Natural Resources. Being that one of Jay's great grandmothers on his father's side was a member of the Ottawa band of Chippewa Indians, the family felt a certain tenuous entitlement to venison.

"Here in Milwaukee, we have the building to attend to and papers to write," Jay focused on the moment again, as if to convince himself, "so even if we could have borrowed or rented a car, the long winter's trip would require more effort and cash than we can afford right now. And then there would be the possibility of a blizzard, and then what about our Kewaunee boiler?"

"And who would get Mrs. Grant her lamb-chops-dearie-from-the-loin?"

When classes ended for the Christmas Break, Jay sent a package with a set of sketching pencils for his sister and a box of chocolates for his grandmother. Lily created a necklace for Violet, made with bright, randomly strung Czechoslovakian glass beads that were sold at the Ben Franklin Dime Store for the ridiculously low price of ten cents a strand. Of course, they were randomly strung and had to be restrung on fishline in an esthetic manner but could be transformed into something quite charming. "One of these days, I will meet you in person, Violet," she muttered as she wrapped the necklace in holiday paper. "I hope we get along because we are family and we both have a certain affection for this Blue Jay guy." Jay also tucked in a picture of The Hatchling for his parents. He knew his mother would hang it on the bulletin board near the doorway at the restaurant.

Lily noticed his pensive mood and delivered a quick kiss on the top of his head. "I guess you're feeling down because you didn't go to the Spiro T. Agnew Anti-Military Ball and Peace Festival last weekend," she attempted to joke. "You missed out on the Weatherman Christmas Caroling."

To further try to lighten his mood, she began singing in falsetto, "I'm Dreaming of a White Riot.... I hear they wowed the crowd. Maybe the Poets for Peace could have done a few numbers."

Jay forced a little smile accompanied by a shrug. "Let's see. How about "God Rest Ye Merry Weathermen, Let peace signs you display...." Lily grimaced—not at the words, but because Jay could not carry a tune.

"You missed a great opportunity, home with your nose in a book. But it's not too late to make amends. Let's make our own party! A good party will cheer you up. You can invite your Poets group and I'll ask all the tenants I know, and a few friends from my seminar. Since we live in this English basement, let's have a Boxing Day Party. December 26 falls on a Sunday."

Lily, as usual, began hatching plans. The enthusiasm in her voice did not strike a bright note with Jay.

"Yeah. With our luck, a couple of the guys from Apartment 6 would want to have a stoner boxing match."

"Well, maybe then we should serve punch and let them get punch drunk. You could be the referee."

Jay's resolve began to weaken. "Um, if we do this crazy thing, let's not call it Boxing Day. Maybe we should just call it a Holiday Open House," Blue Jay volunteered, his spirits rising a bit.

"No! I know! Better yet! Let's have a Holiday Soiree. I've always wanted to attend a soiree," Lily countered. "We'll keep it simple. Just punch and appetizers as evening falls."

December continued to be busy, with many assignments catching up with Lily and Blue Jay that had been put off for the break. Removing the wax from the U-pipe under the sink in Apartment 6 took the better part of a Sunday afternoon that should have been devoted to studying, but Blue Jay went to get some information and tools from Ernie, the caretaker down the block.

"Wax in the pipes?" He shook his head incredulously when Jay told him about the job he was going to undertake. "Candle wax? What kind of idiots do you rent to?"

Ernie was a good mentor, only too happy to offer advice, along with a large wrench and a big tube of some gooey substance. "This here is what you call pipe dope," he explained. "You've got an old building with old plumbing. Turn the nut gently or you might have a bigger mess on your hands than you've bargained for. Once you get the damn pipes apart, be sure the joints are dry. Them smear this dope around the threads before you put it back together."

Jay nodded and thanked him, secretly hoping he could figure this out.

"If you need any help, kid, just give me a call. I'm only a block away."

"Thanks, Ernie. You saved my skin again."

The repair was accomplished without further damage. "I have to make this bad pun," he whispered to Lily who was assisting. "Pipe dope for the pipe dopes."

"We better finish up fast or we'll get high just by breathing the air up here. Wanna keep a piece of the wax as a souvenir?"

"No, thanks. I already have enough in my ears,"

As THEY WERE LEAVING Apartment 6, Moisette popped her head out of the back door of Apartment 5, like a cat waiting to pounce. "Well, hello, you lovely twosome! I want to let you know that we have no more mice, but I saw two centipedes coming up the drain in the kitchen sink yesterday."

"Well, we just took care of a major clog next door. That's enough plumbing for one day," Lily smiled defensively.

"May I suggest a little baking soda down the drain and run the hot water for a few minutes," added Jay. "And if that doesn't work, maybe you can catch some and put them in a fruit jar and keep them as pets."

Moisette actually laughed at that. "Hey, guys, I was just kidding." She closed the door.

• • •

The Civil War of Heat between Generals Grant and Davis continued to rage with almost daily phone calls and verbal skirmishes until Lily had the bright idea of shutting off some of Mrs. Davis's radiators, thus improving everyone's work and sleep schedules in the fine English basement apartment. Lily realized that having the blue wall phone installed in the kitchen just outside the nursery had been a mistake, but it was something they had to live with.

On the afternoon of December 17, Jay came in, tossing down his book bag and stomping snow off his boots. He was laughing his hearty laugh and picked the Hatchling up, folding Lily and the toddler in a big bear hug. "I kindly request a date with you tonight, Dear Lily, in front of the TV after this little one is asleep!"

Lily rolled her eyes.

"Gotta watch the Johnny Carson Show. You know that singer with the ukulele and the Captain Hook nose and the falsetto voice? Tiny Tim? The *Tiptoe Through the Tulips* guy? He's getting married tonight on national television."

Lily burst out laughing. "*You* wanna watch television? That's a first. Sure!"

Jay and Lily settled in on the wicker couch that night, their eyes on the tiny black-and-white screen in the corner of the room. The marriage ceremony they viewed was a strangely solemn affair with a real clergyman, traditionally filled with the King James Bible's *Thee's* and *Thou's* and admonitions to be slow to anger and not puffed up. The bride, Miss Vicki, was bedecked and veiled in white; the groom refrained from using his falsetto voice during the ceremony, and at the end they shared a chaste kiss, followed by a camera shot of Johnny Carson and live audience applause.

"Well, there. We saw it," Jay said. "If I weren't so beat, it would call for a poem." He yawned.

Lily couldn't stop laughing. "Unreal! Be nice to me or I'll buy you a ukulele for Christmas. Wanna take a bet on how long that marriage will last?" Lily countered.

"That was pathetic Hollywood blarney. That's the point I keep trying to make about television. Our simple courthouse wedding had more meaning than this charade." Jay's words hung in the air.

"Well, Jay, you fell for it."

He got up and turned off the television with a dramatic flair. "Let's go hit the feathers and experience reality."

As Lily was vacuuming two days later, she contemplated the wedding of Tiny Tim and Miss Vickie. "Maybe we could expand this idea. Kangaroo courts featuring real kangaroos. Dog weddings. Find a husband for the Lost Lenore, maybe a basset would be nice, and we could rescue one from the pound and name him Edgrrr Poe. Dress them up and marry them off on TV. Thousands of viewers having a little comic relief from ugly news."

The door to Apartment 5 cracked open and Linda invited her in for a coffee break. Lily enjoyed Linda and was thankful for the chance to talk. She knew that the Hatchling was napping with Jay. Linda had been taking some classes at MATC to save on tuition, hoping to transfer to UWM's School of Education after completing her associate's degree.

"How's it going, Linda? I don't see much of you and Sarah."

"We're both busy with waitressing and classes. And Moisette flits in and out. God knows where she goes or what she does." Linda disappeared down the long hall and reappeared with two cups of coffee.

"Sarah should be finished in June. I think she'll stay on here over the summer, though. She's been taking upholstery classes and wants to open a business. MATC put her in touch with some low interest start-up loans. Look at this." She pointed to the floral, high-backed chair in the corner of the living room.

"Not bad!"

"She already has a name for her business: Sitting Pretty Upholstery Shop."

"Maybe Lenny can throw some work her way. How about you?"

Linda shrugged. "One more year to go down there, keeping up the old grade point so everything will transfer. Now I'm finishing up European History from WWII to Present. The professor lives history, makes it real and immediate. Long Polish name, unpronounceable. He has this wild hair and mustache and gestures a lot and talks really fast with sort of a South Side slur. Sometimes I don't even try to take notes—just sit there listening."

Lily nodded. "I wish I had a class like that this time around. I could have used it for my sanity. I have this really pretentious newly arrived professor for my seminar. Ivy League. I don't know who he thinks he has to impress. Not us. People say he's a tough grader. Wants to make UWM the Yale of the Midwest. My other two classes are okay, though. I'm not real interested in statistics. It's required for my Sociology degree. It'll be more fun when I can actually apply it to research."

Linda held up a recent *Life Magazine*. "Have you seen this? Moisette brought it in. It's pretty gruesome." A close-up photo of a deranged-looking man with buggy eyes greeted Lily.

"The Love and Terror Cult. The Dark Edge of Hippie Life." Linda read the headline slowly. They paged through the magazine, gazing at the photographs of cult members living on a ranch in the California desert under the control of a hypnotic leader named Charles Manson.

"The women look like throwbacks to pioneer days," Lily mused, "And the men look just plain spooky."

"They were not harmless crazies riding around in dune buggies playing cowboys and Indians, like the police thought at first. They actually committed those gruesome murders and were trying to start a race war. They almost got away with the murders, but one of the women was in prison for something else and she told another prisoner and they all got implicated."

"I read that last month. Anybody rich and white deserved to be dead, in their book," Lily replied. "Especially rich and white and famous. So much for hippie cults in the desert."

"Things can turn ugly on a dime. Maybe you could research this for one of your sociology classes, Lily. Devise a public opinion survey."

"How could anybody get this far out, and what kind of women would follow orders from somebody like that? Gives everybody in the counterculture a bad name," Lily replied. "And ironically it happened just around Woodstock." She sighed. "I really should get back to work. The dust bunnies are multiplying as we speak."

"I'll bring the magazine down for you guys when everybody's done with it here. Anyway, I always enjoy my little chats with The Hatchling and Lenore."

And with a final sip of coffee, Lily resumed her cleaning duties.

THE HATCHLING DEMANDED INCREASING ATTENTION. He experienced things by tasting them—everything from pencils with enticing erasers to morsels of dog food spilled on the floor. He crawled around the apartment until the toes of his shoes became scuffed and the knees of his jumpsuit became worn. Lenore followed him around, occasionally nudging at him to keep him in some imagined order, until Blue Jay and Lily began to wonder if there were perhaps also some shepherd blood in her. Blue Jay bought The Hatchling a little orange tambourine at the Ben Franklin Dime Store.

Although Lily did not think this toy was baby-proof, Blue Jay tried to teach him to shake the tambourine when he wanted to be picked up rather than crying. "Hey, little Jay-Jay, play a song for me!" he sang to The Hatchling in a loose, nasal imitation of Bob Dylan. "You're not sleepy and there is no place we're going to-o-o-o."

He shook the tambourine and The Hatchling grabbed for it and tried to shake it, too. Now, the real trick would be for The Hatchling to use the tambourine to summon his parents in the middle of the night instead of crying.

Lily went shopping for new tennis shoes but decided to take a sightseeing detour through the basement of the downtown Woolworth's. This was a place of wonder, with gleaming kitchen wares spread out on counters next to discounted towels and linens, next to baby clothes and school supplies. It smelled like a carnival, with the heavy scent of the roasting hot dogs slowly basking on the rotisserie. There was no music, but the shuffle and bang of workers with carts and the subdued conversations of patrons created a dreamy background. As they approached the back of the store, Lily pointed out a large tank of bright goldfish to The Hatchling. She lifted him close to the glass so he could watch them swim.

When the novelty of this wore off, The Hatchling discovered the parakeets nearby. He reached out for one and squeaked. There were perhaps thirty birds in a large wire cage, vivid green and blue, with smart black feathers on their wings and yellow hooked beaks. No sweet music here; they seemed to be communicating in raucous burps while hopping about and occasionally pecking each other or vying for a spot on a little trapeze.

Suddenly it struck Lily. This was the perfect Christmas gift for Mrs.Grant! Shoes could wait. "What do you think, Jay-Jay?" she asked. "Gramma Grant will really be surprised. Which one shall we get her?" Lily observed the interactions among the parakeets.

Since she had been reading Riesman's *The Lonely Crowd* in her Social Order within Human Species class, a requirement for her major, she often thought about "inner-directed and outer-directed" people. "Is it possible," she thought, "that birds and dogs and other species might also have an inner or outer direction? And if so, which type of bird would make the better pet?"

"Outer-directed, of course," she answered herself. "That way, it will actually interact with Mrs. Grant, easing her isolation with its gregariousness. In that case, I should look for the parakeet that is paying the most attention to us."

She stuck her finger in through the bars on the cage. At that point, a blue-breasted parakeet with a slightly manic cast to its eyes hopped over and nipped her finger.

"You're the one!" she laughed, and keeping an eye on that particular parakeet, she rang the bell for service.

"Burp!" it answered.

The Hatchling laughed and kicked in his stroller and tried to reach for the birds. The nearby cages and the packs of birdseed finished off the shoe budget.

The next morning the presentation was made to Mrs. Grant. Lily thought this was something the whole family could do together, but Jay balked at the idea. "How do you know she wants a bird? Maybe you should have asked her first, Lily. Maybe she hates birds."

"Well, in that case, I guess we will have a bird," Lily replied.

With The Hatchling under one arm and the bird in its cage draped with a blanket, she proceeded up the stairs and knocked on the door.

"Um, Mrs. Grant, we have a present for you. We thought you would like this." Lily hesitated, doubting the sense of this gift for the first time. "I can come up and clean the cage if you need a little help," she added.

Mrs. Grant's face broke into an incredulous grin. She graciously received her gift, although seemed somewhat taken aback by its unusual nature.

"Well, Dearie! What a thought! I am sure it must be kept very warm. It is a tropical creature, is it not? We must keep the apartment warm now at all times!"

Mrs. Grant looked around the room and hesitated. "Why don't you just set that cage over here on the buffet close to the radiator? What pretty, bright feathers! And can I get you a cup of tea?"

Lily relaxed. The bird was going to have a good home here. "Sure. I'm on vacation. That little cup in the wires is for water. And I brought you extra seeds, and I can come up and change the sandpaper in the bottom of the cage whenever you call me."

It turned out that this was an anti-social bird that refused to repeat words but chirped in gibberish incessantly all night unless a tablecloth was thrown over the cage. By Christmas Day, it had developed a fine knack for spitting seeds out of the cage. Lily suggested to Mrs. Grant that she name the parakeet Tennis Shoe, since it was bought with money intended for shoes, but Mrs. Grant decided the parakeet was female and named her Messy Bessie.

After returning to the English basement, Lily dashed off a card to her mother, hoping she was still living at the same Tulsa address. "Mama's putting a big kiss in this envelope, Hatchling," she smiled. "This is for your grammy. It might get there a little late, or it might not get there at all, but that's okay."

Christmas Day was a busy time, preparing for the Boxing Day party. Lily had acquired an album by Leonard Cohen for

Jay: *Songs from a Room.* Jay, in turn, presented Lily with Bob Dylan's *Nashville Skyline.* Lily made cupcakes for the soiree, singing along with the album; and also made a small cake for the family, in celebration of The Hatchling's half birthday. They gave him a fuzzy little brown bear. He shook it and tasted its ear, then smiled and said, "Bah!" and made his favorite throaty growl.

That evening, instead of studying, Lily listed all her son's accomplishments in her sociology notebook:

Crawls around on the floor. Interacts with Lenore and all other people. Says, "Hi," Enjoys being read and sung to. Has three teeth. Slurps from a cup. Throws food on the floor when he is full or doesn't like it or wants attention. Puts everything in his mouth. Sleeps with a toy tambourine. Plays peek-a-boo and giggles when you make a face at him and say, "Boo" or growl like a bear. Growls back.

By the afternoon of the Holiday Soiree, the English basement apartment smelled of spruce and twinkled with miniature lights. Blue Jay had found a vintage round oak table cast out at the curbside a couple blocks away and had rolled it home like a big hoop. It now stood draped in a colorful red and green plastic tablecloth, loaded with Christmas cookies, punch, and a crockpot of chili. Artistically arranged around the table were three wooden chairs garnered from the Goodwill Store and toted home on the bus, interspersed with three folding lawn chairs of various styles. The Lost Lenore and The Hatchling, sensing the excitement in the air, scuttled from one end of the hall to the other.

• • •

Over coffee that morning, Jay recalled the generosity of the neighboring building super, Ernie Warner. "He helped us out so much. We just have to ask Klara and Ernie, even on such short notice. This will be an excuse to get Lenore out for a little exercise before the crowds arrive."

Promptly at three, the doorbell rang. Larry and Lenny stood at the door with a bottle of cranberry wine. "How did you know it's my favorite?" Blue Jay asked. "I'm from cranberry country, you know. Upper Michigan. That's about all we can grow in the bogs up there. Along with mosquitos and rabbits and Rudolf the Red-Nosed Reindeer, of course. And frogs...."

Ernie appeared with his wife Klara bearing a plate of Lebkuchen. "This is one of my specialties," Klara announced. "I hope you like them. We had them every Christmas when I was a girl in Germany." The spicy cookies filled the food table with the rich scents of cinnamon and nutmeg. Lily decided she couldn't wait and snatched a cookie immediately.

"Delicious!" Not to be left out, The Hatchling made a grab for it. Klara laughed, "Maybe he could have his own cookie. It's all healthy ingredients."

Next came Mrs. Davis like one of the magi, bearing a large jar of Ma Baensch's herring, her two canes clomping on the wooden floor, followed by Mrs. Grant. While everyone was busy helping Mrs. Grant down the stairs, Lenore took the opportunity to go sightseeing around the neighborhood. She didn't wander very far lest she miss the excitement on her home turf. She did, however, manage to run around the corner and scratch at the door of her poodle friend, who was not receiving guests, and to take a little detour to leave a generous stain of yellow on the neighbor's pristine snow.

She then huddled shivering beside the door until such time that Moisette and Linda arrived, both festively dressed in white satin blouses with long red velvet skirts and capes. Moisette had embellished her outfit with a sparkling tinsel bow and earrings the size of silver dollars shaped like Christmas wreaths. Their third roommate Sarah had to waitress over at the George Webb's, so she sent her regrets; but Linda had baked fudge brownies for the occasion, and Moisette was carrying a large poinsettia.

When Lily opened the door, Lenore lunged inside with a whimper, almost knocking the poinsettia out of Moisette's arms. Lily was startled because she had not even realized that Lenore had gone for a stroll on her own.

Two tenants from Apartment 6, Mel and Dan, sauntered in. They were in jovial moods, reeking of weed. "Scott's coming momentarily," Mel informed them, plopping two bottles of chianti down on the round table, both tenants helping themselves to stacks of cookies, all the while handing out fliers advertising the expansion of the Underground Switchboard. This was a special emergency hotline that desperate hippies or yippies or wannabes could call anonymously for problems ranging from drug overdose, to suicide, to homelessness.

Dan lifted his voice: "You know, we need to get the word out. This group has performed a real community service for a couple years already and now they're expanding into the basement of St. Mary's by the Water Tower. They will have more services, too, even a free clinic."

"Once again I have underestimated the human race," thought Lily, "most specifically at this moment, The Sixes of Apartment Six."

"We pitched in and bought a mimeograph machine. This is the first flier we've printed," Mel boasted. "We're gonna specialize in drug and dealer information. Besides reporting on rat finks and pigs, we are going to research and print information on drugs and let folks know when there's bad shit out there. Gonna call it Weed Sheet."

"I don't think the Civil War Generals will need that," Jay laughed, as Mrs. Grant and Mrs. Davis received the Underground Switchboard informational flyer with puzzled expressions.

"This is a great service," Lily read. "Specially trained phone counselors can offer advice on many troubles and make referrals to professionals if it looks really serious. Says here you can ask about drugs, legal contacts, places to crash, abortion, and anything else that's bothering you. Nothing will be reported to the authorities. They're offering free switchboard training." She paused. "I wish I had more free time. I wonder if you can bring babies along. I would be interested in working for them at some point."

"Much needed around here on the East Side," Moisette observed, launching into a tale of a friend whose parents kicked her out when she came home stoned, and she tried to sleep all night in the Greyhound Bus Station until they kicked her out, too. Apparently she then made her way in the night to Tannenbaum Arms, where she found refuge on the couch the occupants of Apartment 5.

Lily was interested. "When was this? What happened?"

Linda and Moisette exchanged glances. "Last week just at the start of break. It all worked out just fine. She called her brother in the morning and he came and picked her up."

"Um. Actually, she might be coming to the party here tonight. We invited her to crash. Her brother, too," added Linda. "We knew you wouldn't care."

More Apartment Sixers made their appearances. Bongo Bob arrived, with his loopy smile and glazed eyes. He had brought along his favorite ceramic bong, which Blue Jay made him leave in the back hall. Mel had brought along his girlfriend Marsha, who had brought along her guitar and two of her friends, Bella and Ruthie. They were involved in a folk music group and had traveled to Woodstock, enjoying a Summer of Love and Music. After a couple glasses of punch, they filled the room with Woody Guthrie and Joan Baez songs, interspersed with classic Christmas carols.

Mrs. Grant and Mrs. Davis sat side by side on the wicker couch but didn't converse much since both suffered from a bit of deafness. They seemed to be enjoying themselves immensely, as Mrs. Davis tapped both canes to the thrum of the guitar. Moisette adjusted her silver bow and carefully lifted the rhinestone hem of her skirt as she sat beside Mel, trying to enchant him with her news of her upcoming trip to Paris. Mel, however, inched away and kept ogling Bella. All the tenants were present except Mrs. Hopkinson, who sent her regrets along with a crisply folded twenty-dollar-bill as a Christmas bonus.

The Civil War generals seemed to have declared a Christmas truce and left together as evening fell—which is always around four-thirty in late December when the days begin to get longer. The Poets for Peace groupies straggled in and out throughout the evening, replenishing the food supplies on the round oak table with their gifts of wine, home-baked bread, cheese, and cookies. Coats formed a wet, woolen mountain on the bed and Lost Lenore, exhausted from the effort exerted on her neighborhood tour, as well as domestic herding responsibilities, burrowed into the coats and fell asleep. The Hatchling was cooed over and passed around from person to person, eventually falling asleep on Linda's lap.

When the music broke, Larry amused the remaining guests with tales from Milwaukee's past glory when it was marketed to prospective German immigrants as "The New Athens." One Samuel Tannenbaum, disenchanted with the oppressive terms for doing commerce in the Old World, was lured by this propaganda to Milwaukee. Here he established a dry goods store in the area on the east bank of the Milwaukee River called "Juneau

Town." The business thrived, expanding into food and beverages, as well, eventually becoming a stylish "department store.'"

Samuel Tannenbaum became a friend of the Beer Barons, Gustave Pabst and Emil Blatz, selling their foamy product by the bucketful to citizens who found it preferable to Milwaukee water. As the city expanded northward, Samuel's son saw the opportunity to expand the family fortune in real estate holdings; thus, Tannenbaum Arms was erected, eventually given as a wedding gift to Samuel's granddaughter, who had fallen in love with an itinerant stock boy while patronizing the ladies' department of her grandfather's store.

Klara was interested. "I came over from Germany in the 30's. These stories are new to me. Tannenbaum. Do you know, in German that means fir tree?"

Linda nodded. "We are still a German enough city that even our mayor sings *O Tannenbaum* and we light a big tree by City Hall to open the season."

Another glass of punch, another tale... this one, Larry said, was a sad but true holiday story about a schooner that sank in 1912 after leaving Upper Michigan with a great load of Christmas trees. Every year it would travel down and dock in Chicago. The captain would string lights from all three masts, so the ship looked like a giant Christmas tree and put everyone in a holiday mood. Churches and many poor people were given free trees.

"Nobody knows for sure why it sank," Larry added, "but later the captain's wallet floated up."

"That's worthy of a ballad!" Blue Jay interjected. "Somebody should write one."

"*Mais oui.* Maybe you, *mon cher*," Moisette winked. "A little bird told me you're a writer."

"Jay, you're about fifty years behind the times," Lenny laughed. "It's already written."

A refill of the glasses, a toast to the residents of Tannenbaum Arms, and Larry reeled off another ship-sinking tale. "This one," he said, "is even sadder. This explains how the Irish lost their dominant role in Milwaukee politics.

"Um, Larry, maybe not...." Lenny interjected.

Larry stopped abruptly and looked around.

"No! Don't stop!" Lily spoke up. "This is us. This is our history and we should know a little bit of it."

"Have you ever noticed that all the Irish people seem to live in Chicago? The kids don't even go to school on St. Patrick's Day down there. The mayor throws green dye in the river and they have a parade.

"Anyway, in 1860 many of the *best* Irish families of Milwaukee went on a special cruise to Chicago and back on a ship called *Lady Elgin*. There were four hundred passengers from Milwaukee on board. Just think of all those Irish folks, dancing the night away.

"Then a schooner collided with the *Lady Elgin* and it sank! The shore was four miles away and just about everybody died. That damn lake is a cold killer, three out of four seasons. Amen and God rest ye merry gentlemen."

"End of the partiers and end of the tale," said Lenny with a grin.

"Well, let's hope we're not all on a sinking ship of another sort," was Lily's response. "That was a great story, Larry, but let's talk about something more cheerful.

"Sure. How about some of that pound cake? Or perhaps a fudge brownie?" Larry smiled. "And maybe I can persuade you to have a St. Patrick's Party here in March, Lily and Jay. This is a great party space. We could even do gymnastics off the pipes on the ceiling. And I'll have more tales lined up."

"No, I think we should host," interrupted Lenny. "By the way, Lily, I was noticing your ever-so-elegant chair arrangement. If you like, I can get you a matched set the next time I re-do someone's habitat. The trend nowadays is for sleek, sparse lines and people who think they're in the *avant garde* are hiring me to throw out the good old classic furniture from Grandma's attic and replace it with the *moderne* look. Would you like?"

She didn't pause. "I'd like!"

"Well, then, Merry Boxing Day."

"Same back to you."

Shortly after midnight, when all the problems of the world had been discussed but left unresolved, when several fine poems had been read, when all the songs had been sung, the guests claimed their coats and boots and trudged up the back stairs of Tannenbaum Arms as light snow began to fall.

In parting, although all the wine had been consumed, with all the guests' offerings there was more food left over on the table than when the party had begun.

"Oh, Tannenbaum, Oh, Tannenbaum, how lovely are your arms!" Lily sang into the empty hallway as she locked the door and turned off the Christmas lights. Blue Jay had dozed off in his favorite easy chair. Lily tiptoed up and kissed him on his forehead. He did not stir. She sighed. Then, in most uncharacteristic fashion, she reached down and removed his shoes.

In comparison, New Year's Eve was a slow boat ride to China. Both Lily and Blue Jay had research papers to work on, since the semester would come to an end in just nineteen days. "Whoever thought up this schedule is diabolical," Blue Jay complained, looking up from his trusty Underwood Olivetti typewriter. "I wish they would end the semester in December. I am ready for a new start, and this semester is just dragging on."

"Yes, but if we weren't such procrastinators, we could have been out partying by now." She paused. "I can't help thinking.... this year we had Americans walking on the moon. Humans on the moon talking about a great leap for mankind. I'm not feeling it. We had the Summer of Love, but the world showed little love back, even too much hate. Joshua, my dear, what do you think 1970 will hold in store for us?"

"It's a new decade. I'll never stop hoping. Maybe our country will get back on track. End the damn war. Build schools, not bombs. Free college tuition."

"An end to racism. Equality for all."

"Ha! Maybe the Yoopers will find gold in their dead iron mines and it will be the start of another Gold Rush."

"Maybe I'll get a little closer to finishing my degree and find a real research job, Jay. Or maybe I'll take the quick route out and just get certified for teaching. College life gets weirder every day."

"And more imperiled. Maybe I'll get a poem or two published and land a good creative writing fellowship for grad school somewhere like Iowa. At least I have to finish the BA by June."

"Better start applying. Get a positive attitude. Line up those letters of recommendation. Maybe we should go somewhere warm," Lily added. "The Hatchling will walk and talk and grow up in a happy southern place, but we will go up north to Marquette every summer and visit your folks and go on hikes along Lake Superior and you can teach The Hatchling about his one drop of Ottawa blood.

"Up there, Lily—it's God's country. It's home. For me, Lake Michigan just can't match Lake Superior. Lake Superior is alive.

Sorry. Don't get me started on that." He smiled and reached for her. "Happy New Year, Lily, my love!"

"Happy New--."

At that moment the doorbell rang insistently, repeatedly. Blue Jay sighed, "Let's play Guess-which-Tenant-is-Locked-Out."

Just then, they heard the jingle-jangle of a little tambourine from the nursery.

"Oh, no! He heard the doorbell, too! But the tambourine! He's learned it! I taught him that!" Blue Jay beamed.

CHAPTER 5
JANUARY

Wherein the caretakers of the English basement apartment successfully finish off the semester at UWM, but face ongoing challenges with caretaking, parenting and academics. Jay shares a true Pandora's Box story from his Ottawa heritage. Frank visits in the night. Jay sells blood. The choppy sea of political and social turmoil continues to churn around them.

THE PERSON STANDING outside their door at exactly 12:13 AM on New Year's Day was not a keyless tenant, but Frank Baranski, member in good standing of the Poets for Peace; although he was at present abandoning the call of the poet, in the midst of working on a novel. His black ringlets had escaped from his ponytail and his beard seemed to have the remains of cheese pizza embedded in it. He looked like a slapdash, black, smiling angel.

Blue Jay laughed, "C'mon in, Franko. Thought you were a tenant. Good luck for me. You're the first visitor to cross the threshold in 1970."

"I was walking by on my way home from Downer. Not in the mood for big partying. Noticed all your lights were on, so I thought we could share some holiday cheer!" He pulled a partly-consumed bottle of vodka out of his parka pocket.

"Lily?" he nodded in her direction. "A little swig of Poland's best?"

"No, thanks. Another time." Lily sighed, realizing it was going to be a long night, and went to retrieve Little Jay, who had given up on the tambourine and had resorted to his customary wailing.

"C'mon, Hatchling. It's the new year already. Let's leave those guys to do their guy talk. It's definitely time for beddie-bye." She scooped him up and called Lenore. "Snuggle time."

She yawned. "Let's sit in the rocking chair and you can fall asleep again. Let those guys talk all they want. Let them create vodka-inspired metaphors that turn into nothing but wispy, whispered alcohol breath. Frankly, they can have a Frank talk. Josh. Joke or gently tease. I think that's a good name for a baby bird, too. Works for your daddy.... I hope you don't grow up hating your name...." Lily's thoughts began an undisciplined ramble as mother and child fell asleep in the nursery rocking chair and Lenore stole back to plunk down on the floor next to Frank.

Seated in recycled lawn chairs at the vintage round oak table, Blue Jay and Frank lifted their paper cups of vodka to toast the new decade. "*Sto lat!* That's a Polish toast. *May you live to be a hundred!*" Frank intoned.

"And may you be in heaven a hundred years before the devil knows you're dead!" Blue Jay responded. "That's Irish. And speaking of the devil, I'm almost done with *The Tragedie of Joanie Fist.* My semester writing project, based on the Faust story. Faust is German for fist; and instead of Johann, it's Joanie. Righteous Joanie sells her soul to the devil for fame and financial gain, but lives to regret it. I'm reading parts of it in our creative writing seminar next week. It's a little nerve wracking. Professor Wiegner is a tough critic. I'm sweating it. I need an A if I want to get into any grad school writing program."

"The writer's life is tough in general." Frank sighed, taking another sip of vodka. "Selling your soul to the devil? Don't all of us writers do that? Sure, I'm first of all a writer, always will be, but I'm switching my major to public relations and business. Anything my pa thinks is impractical, no tuition comes outta his pocket. It's okay. I can still write. I'll be able to pull a regular paycheck." He paused. "Like Kafka. A postmaster by day." He paused.

"I'm going to have to decide pretty soon if I should enlist or try to get into a graduate program. I'm not against the army. Just against *that* war. If I enlist with a business degree, I think I could request West Germany or Italy. Maybe travel around on my breaks."

Jay shrugged. "You're already in school. You have a safe draft number. Just stick with school, is my advice."

He nodded as Frank re-filled their paper cups with vodka, draining the bottle.

"By this time next year, where will we be, Blue Jay?" No. I'm serious, man. It'll be a whole new scene for both of us." Frank paused. "Let's stay in touch."

"Agreed. Who'd proofread my work and give me straight feedback? Sometimes I look at what's going down around here and think I should just move us to the Upper Peninsula. But that would last about a couple weeks before I'd get the urge to run; and even if I wanted to stay, I doubt that Lily would last that long."

Jay often found it hard to talk about his personal past, but the alcohol talked too. It urged the words to spill out. "I wanted to be a writer since it dawned on me that I could write my way out. I was fifteen when I found my role model. My parents usually never looked past the doorway of their restaurant, but in March of '59 they closed the restaurant for the morning and took my sister and me to Ishpeming. We waited for a Hollywood Special train. Then it hissed and squealed into the station and out stepped Jimmy Stewart and Otto Preminger and all those other stars to make a movie, *Anatomy of a Murder*. Everyone in the crowd was breathless—*oohed* and *aahed*. Me included."

"Heavy. It's another country up there!" Frank lifted his paper cup, which was on the verge of disintegration. "To decaying movie stars and the ghosts of Christmas past! Or as Old Pa said and still says, '*Na z'drowie*!' To your good health."

Jay nodded, "Thanks," and lifted his cup again. "A few years before, there had been a big scandal over a murder. An army dude went deranged when a bartender raped his wife. One of our local luminaries defended him and got him off, and then wrote a book about it—which I had to sneak out and buy because our library banned it. Then Hollywood picked up on it and descended upon us and made notorious half-truth into something glorious."

Frank laughed. "Keep consuming that vodka, pal. It's loosening your tongue. Not too much, though, or it will loosen your guts."

Jay continued, "He published the book under a pseudonym, even though we all knew he was John Voelker. He lived in this huge Victorian house in Ishpeming that we could have fit about ten of our houses and the restaurant into. Other people looked at his place and thought, 'What a great lawyer;' but I looked at it and thought, 'A smart man who wrote a book lives here. Someone from the UP is a famous author. It's possible.'

"I was already keeping secret poetry notebooks, but at that point I began scouring the dictionary for new vocabulary words and making it an issue to excel in English classes. Thinking back, I sure was obnoxious. I came down here after I graduated and started taking classes at UWM, off and on, and now here I am going on seven years of part time classes, ready to graduate. Amen!"

"Such a whiz kid. Ready to age out of the draft, even."

"I'll drink to that. Hand over the bottle."

"Sorry. We finished it off."

"And then there's something else weird. I always knew from my Grandma that I had a few drops of Ottawa blood in me, even though my father chose to ignore this in favor of his Finnish and Irish ancestry. I took a pen name in high school, Blue Jay Hawk. The name just popped into my head.

"But when my grandmother died, I was helping sort through her stuff and I found this old book, *History of the Ottawa and Chippewa Indians of Michigan.* My grandma had written inside, 'Book written by my great, great grandfather, Chief Andrew J. Blackbird, descendant of the Hawk clan, the Pe-pe-gwen tribe, called the Undergrounds. His parents were taken captive out west by the Ottawas after a great battle and were adopted into the Ottawa tribe.' I rescued this book from the trash pile where my father had put it. I read the whole thing and I always keep it in my top dresser drawer under my socks. *Pe-pe-gwen* is a kind of small, ferocious hawk. How did I know to give myself that name?"

By this time, both young men were afflicted with the garrulousness that sometimes occurs with the consumption of too much vodka, and the tales continued.

"I have a story, too, Bro," Frank said. "How do you think a black woman from Arkansas and a Polish man from Warsaw ever got together? I guess they just thought at first that the married life would be one long honeymoon on the moon. Had to find out the hard way. I found out they had a dispute about what to name me when their surprise came--Rufus or Frank. Learned to compromise. Managed to hold it together. Franklin Rufus. Did you know my middle name is Rufus?

"They wouldn't go to Poland. Couldn't go South. My grandpa came North to take care of me while both my parents worked day and night. Best thing that coulda happened. I called him Big Man and he called me Little Man. He was my preschool and my kindergarten and my Bible School. Cabrini-Green didn't really like any of us and we-all didn't like being there, but we had no other plan at first. The Polish grandparents disappeared back behind the Iron Curtain. Not exactly doting over their little Black grandbaby. Now you see me sitting here."

"Living to tell." Jay nodded.

"Being a 'hood baby toughens you up. A fighter. Some street friends turn into junkies with big cars and you don't know them. I had other plans. My Big Man steered me straight. Right now, everybody has a shitload of anger. Black. White. Nam. Pigs. Panthers. Draft. Daftness. Deafness. Slurs. Slaps."

He punched Jay on the knee, laughing. "Imagine the look on a potential boss's face when a guy named Frank Baranski shows up for the job interview. The boss thinks it's gonna be a brawny white Polack boy, and it's scrawny black me! Fuck that shit!"

"We have to keep the volume down so we don't wake The Hatchling!" Jay cautioned.

"Water off a duck's back. Never apologize. Just be your best self and move on. We moved up to Cudahy when I was nine. Big Man said Chicago was as far north as his feet could go and went back to Arkansas. My pa landed a job at Laddish in the core-making department with a decent enough wage and my ma finally could stop cleaning offices every night and put her feet up. Now she enjoys living in her little American Dream bungalow and Pa just keeps putting in the hours to make the mortgage. I look at them sometimes. How they stick together.

Ready to smile at each other over breakfast. Shit. Piece of cake, but not my party."

"Far out! And here we are together. On this day. At this time. 1970. In this place. Tannenbaum Arms. I don't have any answers, but I hear you. I feel it. I'll drink to that, Franko!"

"I'll drink to that, Blue Jay Hawk!"

"Here's to the new year!"

As the vodka was finished, so were their tales—but for that night only.

~

New Year's Day was crisp and bright, but Blue Jay lay moaning in bed. "Coffee! Coffee!"

Lily laughed, "It's almost noon, and I would say you got what you deserved. How late did Frank stay last night? I fell asleep and didn't even hear him leave."

"We spoke of many things. I didn't even look at the clock. Good vibes. I think it was around three or four. How would you feel about living in Ishpeming?"

"Brrrr. That's my answer. Don't even think about it."

The day passed uneventfully with a very late breakfast, studying, defrosting the refrigerator, and organizing. Several boxes still needed sorting and unpacking since their September move, and Lily resolved to get the year off to a good start. Blue Jay recovered enough to clean the front hall, empty several buckets of trash, and check the water level on the boiler. Then it was back to *The Tragedie of Joanie Fist*, which needed only to be proofread and tweaked into final form.

When it was her turn to use the faithful Underwood-Olivetti typewriter, Lily put the finishing touches on her final paper for Dr. Milton's seminar analyzing Puritan attitudes towards wealth and morality and their present-day ramifications in American society. Even The Hatchling was relatively mellow, perhaps enjoying the fact that both parents were home at the same time. They put up an expanding gate for a barricade and kept him confined in the living room where they worked.

"So, what are your thoughts on the Puritan ethic, Blue Jay?" she asked over a supper of leftover spaghetti. "What do you think of this?" She read in a poorly-rendered 1600's pastoral English accent: "*For wee must consider that wee shall be as a city upon a hill. The eies of all people are upon us.*"

"Do you really want to know?" he asked.

"Yes, really."

"Puritan ethics is an oxymoron. I've been thinking about a story from my great, great, however many great grandfather's book. He wrote about the English. Maybe not John Winthrop's Puritans, but English. Later in the early 1800s, I guess it was, during the French war with Great Britain. Some of the Otttawa tribal leaders were summoned to Montreal by the British. They were given a tin box to take back home with them. They were told that there was a treasure in it that should not be opened until they returned home.

"They obeyed this great English chief," Blue Jay continued, a bitter edge creeping into his voice, "and when they got back to their familiar tribal Lake Superior peninsula, they summoned their people and opened the box.

"Inside the box was a smaller box, and inside that box was another box. There was a box in a box in a box. And inside that box, was there a gift? Only little crumbly, moldy pieces of something. Then they all took sick and many, many died. Entire lodges filled with corpses with no one to bury them. Others had to live out their days with terrible round scars all over their faces and bodies. The gift was smallpox.

"And you're asking me what I think of these ethics. Fuck Puritan ethics. What an ugly Pandora's box."

"Ancient Greece, Canada.... My God, Jay, you never told me about this before."

"There's still a lot you don't know. It's not always in the front of my mind, but after Frank and I talked last night..."

"But that was then and this is now. 1970. What are your thoughts on now?"

"And are any of us any better? Have humans learned anything from all the evil and suffering that's already been perpetrated and endured? Breaking into an apartment and shooting a man in his bed? Butchering pregnant movie stars? Trouncing over helpless people and bragging about body counts? Dropping poison gas on villages of innocent people? You'd think we could have come up with a better world than this."

Jay might have continued, driving them both deeper into despair.

Aware of this, Lily sighed. "Hey, Blue Jay, not to change the subject, but we haven't sold our blood for a while. If you're feeling up to it, let's go to the blood bank tomorrow and get some money for second semester books. Let's concentrate on the issues we can actually do something about."

"That's my point, exactly. I hope The Hatchling will never have to sell his Rh-negative blood!"

"Our slogan could be *Rh-Negative Blood for Books*."

"Blood money. How did two negatives find each other? And do two negatives make a positive?" she replied.

"Hey, Lily, you're just too clever for words," he smiled. "I think I married you for your sense of humor."

"Well, Blue Jay Hawk, you certainly don't have to worry that I married you for your money."

• • •

The Blood Center was a long bus ride away, on a neglected street with many boarded up shop windows. A large sign across the front identified it, flanked by a generic red cross on either side.

Inside, all was business to the tune of Muzak. There were white walls, white floors, the strong odor of disinfectant. Reclining chairs were draped in white sheets and an aura of sterility prevailed.

Blue Jay had talked Lily into staying home with The Hatchling; children were not allowed. Jay wished he could just go to the regular blood bank and donate, but the $20 paid for Rh-negative blood at this alternative site would be a transfusion to the budget.

He checked in, showed his driver's license; having previously given blood, there was no extensive paperwork. As he was directed to a chair and the needle inserted, he closed his eyes. Before him, he could see Lake Superior with the eyes of his heart. He felt drawn back; he stood on an eroded embankment, studying the root formations that had been stripped of their soil, looking like powerful sculptures of endurance. The lake roared, whispered some message in a hushed language he strove to understand, but could not.

"Mr. Haakens," he heard his name called sharply.

The reverie was over. A plastic bag filled with precious garnet liquid bulged on the metal frame beside him. He collected his cash and waited in the cold for the bus that would bring him back to the East Side. Since the entire ordeal had taken less than an hour, he was thankful he could use the same transfer.

~

On impulse, Jay got off the bus on Brady Street, a few stops earlier, to pay a visit to Interabang Book Shop, just south of Brady on Warren. He needed a used copy of *Aristotle's Poetics* for a second semester class. He ended up browsing through the stacks longer than he intended, unable to resist battered copies of Ginsberg's *Howl* and Milwaukee poet Barbara Gibson's *Our Bedroom's Underground*, as well. He and Lily read Barbara's frequent articles in *Kaleidoscope* and respected the Gibsons for what he regarded as their radically poetic lifestyle, as embodied in their poetry. "Lily will enjoy the Gibson book, too," he justified the additional spending. "And the underlined passages in the Ginsberg will challenge us to figure out why the reader marked them.

"Interabang. Question mark, exclamation point. I guess the name fits the place. I love the peculiar smell inside bookstores. Emanates musty, papery allure. The power of words. Much going on here at once; some thoughts to question; some to exclaim over."

A mustachioed man entered the store, dressed in a tattered wool English duffel coat. His large Russian fur hat with earflaps clung to his unruly hair like a helmet, giving him the look of a diplomat who had wandered in from a past century.

"His Nibs, George Sharkey!" Jay noticed that he greeted a man who had been arranging papers on the counter.

"Polish George in the flesh!" was Sharkey's response. "Here. Take one. Or maybe two. I know what you're after. Add these to your treasure trove."

The diplomat raised his hand in a fist salute. "Many thanks, my good man!"

Jay noticed the colorful mimeographed newsletter, filled with what seemed to be deliberately pranksterish spelling and typefaces, that Sharkey pressed into the man's hand.

Sharkey then turned his attention to Jay, as if seeing him for the first time. "Take one. It's free. Judging by your choice of reading material there, I'd say you're ready for this. I'm the editor of *Street Sheet*. We're publishing three times a week now. All the latest narc and drug news right off the street, along with helpful hints on communal life and healthy recipes and protests. Courtesy of your local anarchists, YIP, the Youth International Party."

He smiled. "And that's Polish George. He's into historic documents and collects everything counterculture. I'm Pat, otherwise known as George Sharkey. Or maybe I'm George Sharkey, otherwise known as Pat. This coffee can here is for donations, and this other one is for readers to submit news bulletins or stories in general. You can be anonymous or give your name."

Jay grabbed a copy and plunked a quarter into the can. "Thanks. I hope you plan to distribute this around UWM. We need it."

"Ubiquitous! We are ubiquitous!" AKA Mr. George Sharkey replied. "Hang on to this." He paused. "And here." He reached under the stack. "This is an old one, but it's a copy of Volume 1, Number 1. Frame it. It marks a turning point of people's history."

"I'm sure our paths will cross again. Thanks," Jay replied.

Classes resumed after the break, along with ongoing political troubles, just as they had ended, as if there had been no holiday break. With two more weeks until first semester final exams, Jay thought the unrest was escalating. There had been a fire in the basement of Mitchell Hall, but it did not spread upstairs. The fire department and UWM made a big deal of saying it was not arson, but then a few days later Jay picked up a copy of the *Kaleidoscope* and noticed a letter purporting to be from "The

Intergalactic Conspiracy for Cosmic Consciousness" claiming responsibility to "avenge the death of Fred Hampton, the Black Panther Leader."

Jay felt this might be closer to the truth. He had lost much trust and respect for the administration, but at least they were not blaming anyone willy-nilly. "I'm going to be so glad to get out of this place," he thought. "Just one more semester! If it actually was an attempt to burn down Mitchell Hall, at least it was a failed attempt. But what about next time? Will there be a next time?"

Some students wanted to *bring it on and bring it all down*, but other students were on edge, thinking that increasingly violent protests could be imminent. What would destruction of property prove, that taxpayers would just have to spend money on repairs? Jay mused.

As for the faculty, they were under tight administrative scrutiny. Jay's favorite creative writing teacher, Dr. Kathleeen Wiegner, had been denied tenure. The Poets for Peace group had unanimously signed a letter of protest but received no reply. Granted, she hadn't published any articles in academic journals, but she had started an alternative-press poetry magazine and had used her writing talent to oppose the war. Students regarded her as an excellent teacher and mentor. Her encouragement of student writers was well-known.

Other professors were likewise under scrutiny, including the two English profs, known as "The Gibsons;" and one of Lily's former sociology professors, who was suspected of encouraging draft dodgers. An article in *Kaleidoscope* warned about the presence of narcs in classrooms, hired by Police Chief Harold Brier, ready to turn in faculty and students alike. This fueled further feelings of disorientation and paranoia.

It was an open secret that professors had been ordered to stand their ground academically. "Give no leeway to students who skip class during protests." Faculty members were encouraged to keep close attendance records, even to give pop quizzes on light attendance days. Jay discovered there would be a big change in operations in his German class. His professor announced that those continuing with his class during the spring semester would have to abide by the following policy: Three or more unexcused absences during the upcoming semester would result in a lowered grade. Five or more would be an automatic course failure. That had been met with grumbling in the classroom. "Does he think he's teaching high school?" But the real reason was clear, and Jay noticed a tremor in his teacher's voice.

The first semester had seemed to drag on forever, but finally came to a lurching end. Exams went well, as did the presentations of Blue Jay's epic tragedy and Lily's term paper on *Manifestations of the Puritan Ethic in Present Day America.* Students were enthusiastic about Lily's presentation and a lively discussion ensued. Lily asserted that, as in Puritan times, many people still seemed to view the US as "the city on the hill," with a crusading need to impose its values on the rest of the world. To further strengthen her assertion, she had interviewed classmates about their views toward the role of American leadership. Several students spoke of the connection between the early days of the country and what was happening now with US involvement in Vietnam.

Professor Milton said little during the discussion, but listened intently, occasionally nodding and smiling. Lily was sure he was impressed with her work.

Professor Milton was a recent arrival from the East Coast. Administration let it be known that he was a great catch for the university. He vowed to make UWM "the Yale of the

Midwest." As students were leaving, he asked Lily to stay for a moment.

"It's about your paper, Mrs. Haakens," he said pointedly. "Please have a seat here at the front by my table."

Lily obliged.

"I want to give you some feedback. You've done some original research here and the paper is well organized. You write very well for a *woman*, but I make it a point never to give a *woman* an *A*." And with that, he penned a large B+ upon the top of her paper.

Lily felt the floor fall beneath her feet. She drew a deep breath. "I will not let myself cry. I will not curse him to his face." She wanted to raise her voice and confront him with the unfairness of his action, but she caught herself and pursed her lips. She knew she had no recourse; there was no fair system of arbitration in place for handling problems like this. A ruling would always fall in favor of an esteemed professor who could find something wrong with anything when pushed against the ivy-covered wall.

"I can't burn my bridges," she thought, biting her tongue. "If we end up staying here, I will need financial assistance for the fall semester. I have to keep my cool."

With tears of rage just behind her eyes, she spoke, "Thank you for the compliment on my writing." She grabbed her backpack and left the classroom without looking back.

In the hall, half blinded by tears, she almost bumped into a fellow classmate, one of the few women in the same class.

"So, Lily," she said. "I waited for you. I noticed he called you back."

"Viola!"

"He's a bum. A womanizer. Did he try to feel you up?"

"Um, not that kind of bad," Lily replied.

"I heard from some other students that he likes skinny

women with big boobs. Thought he might have tried something."

"No, but I met another side of his piggery. Amazingly ironic, since it was following a presentation of my paper on the Puritan ethos." She explained the situation to Viola.

"Well, my women's consciousness raising group is keeping lists against professors for this kind of thing. Eventually we will figure out how to make administration listen. We're compiling a file on him, in case you'd like to add to it. Of course, he'd deny everything, but you aren't the first person to have a grudge against Dr. Ivy-League-of-the-Midwest. He thinks he's God Almighty. Bet his penis is the size of a toothpick and he feels he has to compensate. Or maybe he was low man on the totem pole at Yale and he's taking it out on us Midwesterners."

"Thanks,Vi. You should be majoring in psychology, not sociology. That makes it a little better. B+. Bad scene. I'll never take another class from him. I swear."

"Never give up. Never give in. I'll keep in touch." She embraced Lily and departed. "Peace!"

LILY WALKED QUICKLY through the dusk. The edges of the snowbanks had melted during the day, but now were beginning to re-freeze, creating intermittent gleaming pools of black ice on the sidewalk. The cold felt welcome; a light sleet had begun to fall, its biting numbness kissing her face. "The Eskimos are supposed to have thirty-seven words for snow," Lily grimly reminded herself. "I wonder what little spits of ice are called. Maybe *Sky Tantrum.*" She resolutely trudged on.

The inevitable meltdown came as soon as she entered the refuge of their doorway beneath the fire escape—the front door of their home. "What do you think, Jay? I think I have every right to have a sky tantrum! I write very well, *for a woman.* That's what Professor Milton said about my paper. All that work I put into it! I should have known better. I was doing fine in the Sociology Department until they knew I had The Hatchling. *For a woman.* Does a woman get locked in the ivory tower like some poor Rapunzel who is ordered to let down her hair and then gets punished for letting down her hair?"

Blue Jay gave her a great bear hug. "Don't worry. You can finish up this semester and shake the dust off your sandals if you want. That's what my mom would say, and she's had it worse than any of us. Just shake the dust off."

Lily smiled, "Or the snow, as the case may be. But it's not as easy as you make it sound. I'd rather fight. I am a fighter, you know. A guerilla. No, maybe a gorilla, swinging from trees." She glanced up. "Or from these infernal heat pipes all over the ceiling."

"Keep your options open. Time is on your side. You can always switch your major or switch schools if they try to pull any shenanigans here. Anyway, who knows where we'll be in the fall."

"Get those applications going, Blue Jay. I'll just sit here and let my anger boil. Maybe I'll write an anonymous letter to *Kaleidoscope*. Or hell! Sign my name in capital letters."

"Hey, sign your name. I'll back you. 100%." Blue Jay paused and smiled, "Aren't you the formidable lady who got 97% on her boiler operator's test?"

"Right on! I'll sleep on it."

"That's the spirit!"

~

THERE WAS a three-day hiatus between semesters, during which time the building was given a thorough cleaning and the loads of laundry washed. The Hatchling was taken in for his well-baby check-up and booster shots, giving him the opportunity to bellow like a champion, proving that nothing was wrong with his lung capacity. Lily and Mrs. Grant cleaned Messy Bessie's cage and drank mint tea; Lily bought strands of glass beads at the Ben Franklin to make more necklaces; Jay scouted out the bulletin board in the English office and found grad school application forms for Georgia and Iowa and the University of Chicago.

At eight o'clock the next Monday morning, Blue Jay set off for what he hoped would be the first day of his final semester as an undergraduate. Lily had gone to bed with a lump in her throat but awoke at nine o'clock with a bee in her bonnet. "Action," she thought. "I will continue my research and my writing. This is what I love doing and this is what I will continue to do."

She threw off her flannel nightgown. "The old fool even admitted that I write well. Maybe I'll hitch up with W.I.T.C.H. and do women's underground theater. Zap! Make huge, bigger-than-life-size puppets and we'll have a sit-in like everybody else. Maybe...."

She pulled on her favorite comfort garment, a red Bucky Badger sweatshirt she had acquired during her freshman year at UW-Madison. "I've had my head in the sand. They treated me differently here at the university when they didn't know I was a mother."

She fished for clean underwear and socks in the laundry basket. "Puppet shows by Women's International Terrorist Conspiracy from Hell! I'll do it!" Lily indulged in her occasional habit of delivering soliloquies when she was upset. Putting on her worn tennis shoes, she added, "That is, if W.I.T.C.H. will take me. Or maybe I will work with that new group Theater X."

She marched into the small nursery off the kitchen where

The Hatchling was beginning to stir. "You are a sleepyhead today, Baby Blue Jay. Rise and shine! Your mommy writes very well....*for a human*!"

Perhaps that very day Lily would have checked around campus for a poster advertising the next W.I.T.C.H. meeting, or she would have begun an all-out campaign to publicize the sexist attitudes prevalent in the Sociology Department. However, at ten o'clock that morning, the phone rang. Mrs. Davis was speaking in her usual deliberate voice. "Lily, I want you to know, Mrs. Grant passed away last night. I noticed her paper was still at the door, so I called her. No answer. Lenny across the hall keeps her spare key, so I told him about the newspaper and he let himself in when she didn't answer the door. He found her in her bed. Looked like she was asleep, so peaceful. No need to involve you. They're coming in about an hour to remove her body. And I notified her daughter in California."

Lily inhaled and held her breath, waiting for comprehension to sink in. "No! It can't be," she inadvertently spoke. *Why does life have to be like this?* Her thoughts tumbled around. *Best not to become too attached to people. But it's my nature to attach. Mrs. Grant was my first friend in this building....*

Mrs. Davis attempted to console Lily. "In my church, it's what we call 'a good death.' I'm sorry. I know she cared very much for you." Lily knew such words of tenderness were difficult for the tough old soldier. She appreciated the kindness.

"Should I come up? Is there anything I can do?" Lily asked, fighting back tears for the second day in a row.

"It's quiet as death up there, except for that noisy bird. Maybe you can take the bird," Mrs. Davis suggested. "She loved that little squawker for as long as she had it, you know. Maybe in a couple days you can help her daughter clear out her things. Let me know if you want to stop in for a cup of tea later."

Mrs. Grant loved this daughter. She had her pictures sitting around everywhere. Finally this daughter is coming to Milwaukee. Why didn't she visit her mother more often when she was alive? Lily paused, separating her spoken words from her thoughts. "That would be nice—later when I come up to get Messy Bessie," Lily replied. "Sure. Thanks, Mrs. Davis. I know you're feeling this, too."

"Hatchling, my dear," said Lily, planting a kiss on his forehead as she replaced the receiver. "Some things are more important than others in this world. Like you. Like Mrs. Grant and Mrs. Davis and your papa. Like love and Lost Lenore and all good lives. Some people like Professor Milton are just plain slow learners. They're not worth wasting your time on." Then after a pause she added, "Except it is not a waste of time to take action against injustice." Another pause. "Remember that, little Hatch!"

Hearing Lily's soliloquy, Lenore sprang to action and began urgently whining at the door.

"Hey, Hatchling, how about a ride in your back carrier? Let's take Lenore out on a potty walk." Lily made every effort to keep the tremor out of her voice as her thoughts turned to the loss of a kindly woman who had become a dear friend.

Winter weather graciously brought a late-January reprieve to the cold tundra in the late morning hours. Although the city had endured a bout of Dutch Elm Disease in the mid-sixties and many mature trees had been slaughtered, the boulevards on the East Side had been re-forested with fast-growing red maples. These trees had been spangled with ice overnight but were now dropping their diamond treasures like gracious ladies-in-waiting in obeisance to their queen. Lily breathed the damp air deeply and concentrated on the future. "No more classes with Professor Milton," she thought. "I'll drop my seminar with him and add something else—maybe a public policy class—while I still can make a schedule change for the new semester."

At eleven forty-seven, Blue Jay left his German class, so lost in his own thoughts that at first he did not notice that Lily, Lost Lenore, and The Hatchling were waiting at the entrance of Bolton Hall. "We decided to walk you home," Lily said. "I have some sad news."

Lenore almost knocked him over, trying to kiss him on his lips.

"Yow! Dog's breath!" he laughed. "So what's to be sad about?"

MESSY BESSIE ADJUSTED WELL to her new home, her cage hanging from a chain looped around a radiator pipe on the kitchen ceiling. Since the kitchen was always the center of action, she chattered away in bird gibberish, always ready to add her comments. When Lenore discovered that this feathered creature would remain out of reach, she showed attitude of species superiority by ignoring the parakeet. The Hatchling loved to pull himself to standing position on the table leg and stare up at it, laughing.

Mrs. Grant's daughter arrived and decided that there would be no funeral; just a simple cremation would do, and the ashes would travel back to California with her. She requested Lily's and Jay's help clearing out the apartment. The woman was elegance personified, from coiffured silver hair to gleaming high-heeled boots. She moved with that same certain grace that her mother had shown, and had that same small, careful hesitance in her speech. "Just call me Leticia, Lily. Mrs. Behrenson is just too formal.

"My mother told me you were a great help to her, Lily," she continued. "I always tried to get her to move to California to be closer to me, but she was set on staying in Milwaukee. As you probably know, my mother could be really formidable. Really stubborn when she dug in."

Lily was surprised to hear that hear that this offer had been made and Mrs. Grant was the one who chose to stay on alone. She resolved not to make so many snap judgments about people from that moment on.

"I don't plan on taking this furniture. I'll just grab the photos and sort through the personal papers. I will have to box and ship the Cruikshank Dickens etchings from the dining room. Then there's that Spicuzza oil painting of Bradford Beach with the Milwaukee skyline in the background that I grew up with—I can't part with that, along with some of Mother's Spode china that was her wedding gift. Anything else you can use, help yourself. The rest can go to the St. Vincent or Goodwill."

Remembering how she had volunteered with meal preparation at Casa Maria Hospitality House during the spring before Little Jay's birth, she asked, "Leticia, is it okay if we call this place that helps a lot of homeless women and children and vets?" Letitia approved without hesitation.

This offer of furniture was exciting news, leading to the familial acquisition of an enamel-topped kitchen table with four red vinyl chairs, a maroon velvet couch, and a Persian carpet for the living room. As they were hauling the goodies down to their apartment, Jay proclaimed, "The prize is this dresser for the Hatchling. I'll paint it bright blue with Lake Michigan scenes and lines from e.e.cummings poems."

Lily and Jay spent their entire Saturday packing up the clothing and dishware and miscellaneous household items. Lily gave Casa Maria a call, and two returned Vietnam vets in a battered pickup truck were only too happy to come by that same evening to pick up the items.

"I misjudged her daughter, Jay. I seem to be good at that," Lily mused. "Letitia seems to be a really independent person, but so was Mrs. Grant, when you think about it. Mrs. Grant had her options. I am glad she stayed here so I got to know her." She paused. "I'm going to miss her presence overhead in Apartment 2."

Letitia departed early Sunday afternoon. She came down the back stairs to the lower level to hand over the keys. Her words of thanks were effusive as the taxi driver out on Cramer Street kept honking impatiently. Lily noticed Letitia's large, plaid travel bag, sure that it contained the canister with the remains of her friend Mrs. Grant. The Civil War of the Heat was over; Lily would miss it for as long as she and Jay and The Hatchling and Lost Lenore and Messy Bessie would live in the English basement of Tannenbaum Arms.

CHAPTER 6
FEBRUARY

Wherein the Grimeses move into Apartment 2, Messy Bessie learns to bark to guitar music, the trial of the Chicago 7 continues with a "not guilty of conspiracy" verdict, and three surprises—two pleasant and one unpleasant—find their way into the caretakers' English basement apartment.

"Well, it would have been nice of Mr. Dreschler to let us know that he was putting a rental ad in the Sunday paper with our phone number!" Lily grumbled as she took the sixth phone call of the morning regarding Apartment 2. "Don't you think you could get up now, Blue Jay? Some people are coming to look at the apartment at one, and you can either show it or take care of The Hatchling and I'll show it."

He groaned, yawned, stretched, bumped his head on the headboard of the bed, and rolled over. It had snowed again and Blue Jay had spent hours on Saturday chipping ice and shoveling. Now his muscles ached and he wanted nothing more than to stay immersed between the warm covers.

"Okay, I'm getting up. Right now." He proceeded to drift into a state of defiant dozing. "Make that in half an hour," he said, pulling the comforter over his head.

The phone rang again and Lily let it ring. She sat in the kitchen and took a deep breath, enjoying the muted reflection of sunshine through snow on the kitchen walls, which she had, in a fit of madness over semester break, painted a vibrant blue. It was as close to Mediterranean sky as she could get, calling back a vague memory of a summer three years ago when she had bummed around Europe on a Eurail Pass, eventually ending up in Crete where she had stayed until the last possible minute. Now snow had drifted against the windowpanes giving them the lazy appearance of half-shut eyes. The old enamel sink gleamed and the coffee pot perked, creating an air of pleasant domesticity; nonetheless Lily always was aware that beyond the walls of their small haven was a greater world where insurmountable problems loomed.

Lily had taken several phone calls that morning and ignored an equal number of others; during the afternoon she and Blue Jay would hold court in Mrs. Grant's now emptied apartment for prospective tenants who expressed interest. Mr. Dreschler expected her and Jay to repaint Mrs. Grant's living room, but that would have to wait for the following weekend. Most prospective tenants seemed disenchanted by the faded spots on the living room walls where pictures had hung. Lily and Jay admitted to themselves that the whole place looked a little dismal and that a coat of paint would help. The overcast sky only added to the gloom, and the memories lingered.

Lily had dreaded returning to Mrs. Grant's empty apartment, with everything removed. It had all happened so quickly, and without warning. It seemed to her that some angel of death had soared down and taken her friend; then Letitia had come like some *deus ex machina*, swooped in, taken matters into her competent hands, erased all traces of a life except for shadows on the walls and indentations in the carpets, and then departed with her mother's ashes.

"This is how it can happen, Blue Jay," Lily said. "Not even a memorial service. I would have felt better if we could have gone to a chapel and prayed and cried together. No closure. Just whoosh! And gone."

"Maybe this is the way Mrs. Grant wanted it. I never knew her to go to church and never saw any church ladies stop by like with Mrs. Davis. Maybe the Grants had their family issues that we'll never know about," Blue Jay responded.

"People are like that. Families are like that. I know, some couples who have fancy weddings and seemingly perfect marriages and perfect children—they're the first ones to fall apart. They're not real. You're the sociologist. You should know this."

"Some get it right. Who knows?" Lily sighed. "But whatever transpired before, I know that Mrs. Grant loved this daughter very much and missed her every single day, and now I know that she had options. But she chose to live life here on her own terms."

"*Quoth the raven, Nevermore,* as Papa Poe said in his sorrow. Bravo for Mrs. Grant. May she rest in peace wherever her ashes end up."

Conversation of this nature continued until the doorbell rang, heralding a long Sunday afternoon of caretaking duties.

Although several people came to look at Apartment 2, some found fault with the gray wall-to-wall carpeting with indentations where the furniture had stood for many years; others wanted the entire place re-painted, still others found it too large, too plain, too shabby. Only one couple found it pleasing, just what they were looking for.

"Do you keep the place warm?" the woman queried. "Is the electricity included?"

"Yes to your first question; no to your second," Lily replied.

"What about a security deposit? When could we move in?" the tall, gaunt man asked bluntly.

"Well," Blue Jay hesitated, "whenever, I guess. You'd have to place a security deposit of two hundred dollars." He looked around the room. "I was planning to paint next weekend."

"That doesn't matter to us," the man hurriedly replied. "You don't have to paint. We'll just hang up some Elvis posters."

"I'll have to notify the property management firm to get their okay. Let me have your name and place of employment. They'll want to run a credit check. I will hold the security check, but it all depends on management's approval."

"Ummm, I'm currently unemployed, but my wife is working. We're the Grimeses, Orville and Sherl," Orville said, extending his hand to Blue Jay. "And this is our son, Travis, named after Elvis Presley's uncle." He laughed nervously. "He's eight. He's quiet, though. He won't bother anybody, I'm sure. Will you, Travis?"

The child remained sullen, staring at the floor. "Why do we have to move again?" he muttered, more to himself than as if expecting an answer. "You can't make me go to another new school."

Sherl Grimes spoke up. She was a small, buxom woman with bright lipstick, gleaming blond hair with dark roots, and an unnatural blush to her cheeks. Her voice had a pleasant Southern drawl. "I am employed as a cocktail waitress down at Frenchy's on East North Avenue so this place would be real handy. I make good tips. Frenchy's is known for elegant dining and big spenders. Our hours work well with parenting; Orville's usually gone days when he's working and I'm gone in the evenings, so somebody's always here with Travis."

Travis glared at her, "I'm grown. I don't need nobody."

Blue Jay grinned. "Oh! Well, whatever works for you. That's cool."

"Orville is expecting to go back to the docks as soon as the shipping season starts. They pay real good, you know. In the meantime, he does a praiseworthy Elvis imitation and is hoping to get a few gigs."

Orville nodded, smiling widely.

"I tried contacting Elvis, but I guess he's just too busy to bother about a little bro from Tupelo. I just hafta keep trying out of adoration."

Sherl quickly added, "He worked on the docks this past summer and even on into October. The life of a stevedore is real feast-or-famine. I guess you could say we're in famine season now."

Orville laughed. "As Sherl mentioned, I *do* play the guitar. But I'm not one of them hairy-faced hippies. No offense."

He smiled at Blue Jay, as if noticing his unruly red hair for the first time.

Jay laughed. This conversation was getting weirder by the moment, he thought.

"Went to the same high school as Elvis Presley. Humes High School down in Memphis. 'Course he was long out of there before I come on the scene, but I've practiced singin' along with his records and I know all the lyrics. I even have a silver-spangled suit that I wear for special performances." He winked. "Elvis can't be everywhere, you know. That gives me a chance to perform. Course, I don't charge as much, either."

"We do have all types of people in this building—young and elderly, hip, yip, straight, and gay. And we all get along." Blue Jay paused for emphasis. "All of us."

The conversation continued along this vein and eventually

the Grimeses filled out the necessary information and left a $200 deposit on the first month's rent.

"See you soon," said Orville, zealously shaking Blue Jay's hand. The Grimses then climbed into their battered yellow Volkswagen and drove off in a puff of exhaust fumes.

Although no one else had expressed the slightest bit of interest in occupying the apartment, Lily and Blue Jay held off contacting Mr. Dreschler until the following afternoon, at which point Mr. Dreschler said to go ahead and turn over the keys to the Grimes couple, since he wanted to be able to collect rent for February.

"Personally, I think if he lets it go much longer, he'd have to give a couple weeks' free rent, and he's too tight-fisted for that," Blue Jay mused. "Well, at least we got out of painting."

Lily felt misgivings about the whole affair. "Blue Jay, there's something strange about these people. I don't know. They're friendly enough, but I just didn't pick up good vibes from them. Maybe it was the way they treated their little boy."

"Hmmm. Different lifestyle. Do you think it's just a North-South thing? I mean, we're not supposed to enter prospective tenants in a popularity contest, and the final decision is Mr. Dreschler's. I guess they're okay," Blue Jay continued. "It's not like all kinds of people are vying for the apartment."

"I wonder what will come of this," Lily sighed.

The new semester brought a change in the childcare arrangement. Lily's schedule was less demanding since she had decided to take an introductory level urban studies class rather than Professor Milton's graduate level seminar—where she was destined to receive no higher than a B+. She was unsure about how to continue her studies, especially since they might be in a different school next fall if Jay could get into a graduate writing program somewhere. Jay had squeaked through the first semester of his German class with a C but would need to spend extra time in a study group.

Messy Bessie seemed to be adapting quite well, and the interactions between Little Jay and the parakeet proved to bring comic relief to Lily's and Jay's increasing feelings of deep despair and disbelief as the United States troops advanced deeper into the Asian jungles. The war protesters continued to raise consciousness on campus, so it felt good to retreat to their subterranean kitchen with hissing steam pipes, chattering bird and babbling child.

Valentine's Day came and went with little ceremony. Lily baked a special heart-shaped chocolate chip cookie the size of a pizza pan. When Jay noticed some special preparations underway, he slipped out over to the supermarket and picked out a single red rose for Lily. They shared a supper with the strains of "Love Me Tender" seeping through the ceiling. "Well, isn't this the height of romance!" Lily remarked, blowing kisses to the Big and Little Jays.

Their personal party was interrupted by Sherl pounding on the door. She wanted to use the phone to call in to Frenchy's to say she had a headache and wouldn't be able to work. "We plan to get our own phone next month. By the way, I hope you don't mind if we gave your number out in the meantime. People might be calling to arrange Elvis gigs. You can just take the number and let us know, just in case."

Jay and Lily exchanged glances. "Well," Lily remarked. "It better be a really temporary arrangement. In case you didn't notice, the phone is right outside the nursery."

Jay shook his head. "Really temporary."

Oblivious, Sherl thanked them. "Sorry. Gotta run!"

BESIDES THE ONGOING protests on campus and the advancing frustration around the war's expansion, Lily and Jay had caught glimpses of the ongoing trial of the Chicago 7. Jay's opinion of television was changing, and he always put aside his studies to catch the ten o'clock news with Lily. There had been special moments of the trial captured on TV that caught his fancy, such as the time Judy Collins was invited into the courtroom by the defendant's attorney, William Kunstler, serenading everyone with "Where have All the Flowers Gone?" Lily sang along.

The trial dragged on with new theatrical adventures airing nightly. Jay was especially delighted when Attorney Kunstler saw fit to examine Phil Ochs, the folk singer who had assisted Jerry Rubin and others in bringing in a live pig shortly before the 1968 Democratic Convention. The Yippie Party named him Pigasus and brought him to the Chicago Civic Center next to the Picasso sculpture where they nominated the pig as their candidate for president. Of course, they were all arrested, even Pigasus. Jay had missed that event at the time, arriving the following day. "Including this event is a stroke of genius on Kunstler's part. Sometimes the best points are made with humor taken to the next level, Lily!" he exclaimed.

That night he stayed up to jot down a poem that was laughing through his brain:

Ponderings of Pigasus

When the day was young
I was happy in my sty,
Bathing in the mud,
Eating table scraps and crud.
Then one day:
Yanked away.

What's going on here?
My pignappers clap when I sing.
I have perfect pitch.
But I miss my muddy ditch:
Oink
Vote for me
To be
Oink
President!
Snort
Those who have slung mud at me,
I thank you.
Those who have taunted me with
Pig, pig, pig,
Boo to you.
Three cheers for your future president!
I do not miss my sty,
Although the food was better on the farm.
Now I am Pigasus the Strong
And I will end all war.
I will bring the troops home.
I will wage peace
And stage Oink-ins
And build huge mud baths in all public parks.
A vote for me is a vote for sanity.
Oink.
Oink.
Oink.

Jay smiled to himself, read it over again, crumbled it up, and tossed it across the floor. "Some poems are just scribbled out for catharsis," he thought. "The world doesn't need another pig poem, but writing it was a trip."

The Lost Lenore thought it was the start of a late-night

game of fetch and leapt off the couch.

Jay laughed. "Let's get you out for a bonus constitutional."

On February 18, good news regarding the verdict of Chicago 7 defendants lightened the mood on campus. A couple hundred students held a noisy, unscheduled Yip-parade around the campus, celebrating the fact that the defendants were found not guilty of conspiracy to incite a riot at the 1968 Democratic National Convention.

One zealous English professor, a fairly new arrival affectionately called "Young Frankenstein" by his students because of his physical resemblance to Basil Rathbone, led his students out into the corridor and he also joined in. As the revelers snaked and pounded their way through the corridors and stairwells of Bolton Hall, Lily observed the goings-on from her classroom with a smile.

It seemed basically just another day in the halls of learning...that is, until Professor Young Frankenstein led his students through a door that stated "Emergency Exit Only" and triggered a fire alarm throughout the eight-story building. It signaled the end of classes for the afternoon. The union commons became a default destination, crowded with students celebrating the wonders of the day.

"I guess the trial outcome is some small vindication." Blue Jay stated, recalling how he had been at the convention as a protester, but thankful he had chosen to withdraw from the crowd when he saw the mounting violence.

"To me the pen will always be mightier than the sword or the teargas cassette. I think there are better ways of expressing opinions. Just look around now. What was accomplished? The war is still going on and protestors are still being clubbed in this country. Even that whole trial turned into a freak show. A big, public circus on national television with both sides making a mockery of the system. I don't know what they were trying to accomplish. Contempt of court? Is this a victory?" His mixed feelings merged into germs of a new poem. He reached into his backpack for his yellow legal pad and jotted down a few lines:

There's a wheel on the circus
That spins round and round in the hearts of the children
Watching the show from the bleachers
With the bear whose ruffles are rags.

LILY SMILED and held her silence. She was accustomed to this type of interruption. When he looked up, the conversation continued.

"Hey, Blue Jay, the whole world watched them bring down the system. Now you're talking like an old man. You know what they say. 'Never trust anybody over thirty.' You've got three more years to be trusted."

"Three and a half. I'm damn sick of this war and all the mess that never quits. Bloody murder. What will this world be like when the little jaybird has to flap his wings and fly on his own? What kind of place will we leave him? Christmas in Cambodia?" Blue Jay bit his bottom lip. "Here's hoping it'll get better."

Although they moved through the rest of the week as if swimming through lead, the following Monday mail brought two surprises. First was a postcard from Jay's sister thanking them for the gifts. "Hope to see you soon!" was added in his father's spidery handwriting.

"Look at this card, Jay. Your sister says it's the Paulding Light. Did you ever hear of that?" Lily couldn't make sense of it.

"Sure. Grew up with it. We used to drive down by Paulding on the old forestry road by the tracks with a six pack and wait for the ghost. I really saw this ghostly light a few times. We all did. For real. The ghost of a dead brakeman is stuck there where he was run over by a train and he comes waving his signal lantern."

He studied the card. "Looks exactly like this. A dismal, abandoned stretch of track with tall trees on both sides with no room for escape, and then suddenly this glow appears in the distance. I'll take you there this summer, Lily."

"Is that a promise or a threat?"

The second remarkable piece of mail was a thin envelope announcing that *The Tragedie of Joanie Fist* was accepted for publication in *Undercurrents*, a national small press magazine held in high esteem by the UWM English department—in fact, by English departments all around the country; although very few other people had ever heard of the magazine outside these learned circles of academia. It was especially important because the entire drama would be printed, filling almost the entire summer edition of the magazine.

Blue Jay's mood shifted. From feeling like he was swimming through heavy metal, he felt he was walking on air. This prestigious publication definitely would enhance his chances for acceptance into a graduate program. "Time to send out my applications," he announced. "Maybe past time," he added worriedly. He had been looking at the University of Chicago and also at Paul Engel's writing workshop in Iowa City. This affirmation of his writing gave him the boost to his self-esteem he needed to actually take action.

Lily took his swollen head in stride, realizing that the victory had been hard fought and, in her opinion, well deserved.

That evening as they were celebrating Blue Jay's victory with carry-out submarine sandwiches, the doorbell rang in its usual raucous fashion. This time it was Larry and Lenny, beaming at them, each carrying two sturdy wooden chairs. "No, we don't have any building complaints. Quite the opposite. We come bearing gifts. I'm working in a mansion over on Lake Drive. Their plan calls for Swedish Modern, but these chairs just seemed too good to throw out. These chairs are a perfect match for your round oak dining room table. We thought you could use them."

"They're beautiful!" Lily reached out to touch the smooth wood.

" Mission style. Well, then, we wish a belated Happy Valentine's Day to the best caretakers this building ever had," Larry smiled.

"Do you have time for coffee? And how about some cookies? We can sit at the round oak table and break in the chairs."

"Break in, but not break, I hope!" Lenny quipped.

"Well, I think we'll have to break Blue Jay of the habit of tilting back and balancing on two chair legs when he's expounding," Lily replied.

A pleasant hour was spent as Larry and Lenny regaled them with more tales from Milwaukee's past. This time they told about the legendary Gertie the Duck who had built her nest on a busy downtown bridge and proceeded to raise nine ducklings, with considerable help from the Milwaukee citizenry. It was during World War II and the people needed something to be cheerful about. Even the newspapers had carried daily progress reports. Lenny had grown up in Milwaukee and his mother had taken him down to the Wisconsin Avenue Bridge near Gimbels Brothers Department Store so he could personally meet Gertie. "Crowds of people quietly, almost reverently appeared every day," he related. "My mother made me walk on tiptoe."

"Maybe we need another Gertie-like diversion," Jay said.

"You'll have to tell this story to him when he's older," Lenny said, nodding at the Hatchling. "There's even a sweet book out. *Make Way for the Ducklings*. I'll see if my mother still has my copy from when I was little. I don't think she ever throws anything out—just lets it stack up, year upon year."

"You might say she lives in a storage bin, Lenny," Larry interjected. "I've seen your mother's place. The stuff is stacked so high that I am afraid to walk through the hall. She must have every scrap of paper she ever got."

Lenny laughed. "And every report card I brought home, and every Valentine and drawing, and even my baby footprints stamped on vellum." He stared at the ceiling, as if seeing his baby footprints tracking around up there. "I worry about a pile of junk collapsing on her as she tries to go from the kitchen to the back door. Maybe we should spend a weekend with her out in Mayville and offer to help her clean it out. I haven't tried for a few years now. Maybe she'd be more receptive now."

"Every time we go there, it gets a little worse. I don't think she can get to the back door anymore." He paused. "Hmm, Lenny. That's probably why you became an interior designer, with all that emphasis placed on the assembling of stuff. But, seriously, all her clutter is just not healthy."

"Don't play shrink-o with me here, please, Larry. What will our young friends here think?"

"We think you are marvelous and very cool and...." Lily continued, "please have some more cookies!"

When The Hatchling began to fuss and Lenore began to whimper nervously demanding her evening stroll, the party broke up. The cookie crumbs found their way to the trash, the coffee cups to the sink, to be taken care of the next day. A dish-towel was thrown over Messy Bessie's cage. The Hatchling fell asleep clutching his tambourine, Lenore sprawled on the carpet next to his bed.

Lights burned late in the English basement apartment, as the evening's dwindling hours were filled with memorizing a list of irregular German verbs and reading Adkin's *Vampire*

Nation: An Analysis of Advertising Practices in America. A little before midnight, Lily yawned and turned in for the night, but Jay put aside the German workbook, took out his yellow legal pad and continued to work on his "Wheel on the Circus" poem.

~

THE PRESENCE of the Grimes family marked a change in the building. In addition to the folk music coming from Apartment 6, there were now the twangs of Orville's electric guitar, which seemed not to have a volume control. Orville offered anyone a tune at the drop of a hat, especially those in his Elvis repertoire. One of his favorite songs was "Old Shep," a ballad about a boy whose dog saved him from drowning and had to be shot by the boy when he got old but went to doggy heaven. Orville assured everyone that Elvis had made this song famous, although no one in the building had ever heard it before. His version of "Love Me Tender" would have shaken the rafters, if there were any rafters to shake. Fortunately, Mrs. Davis was somewhat hard of hearing, and had not called to complain.

The Lost Lenore seemed to take special umbrage at the final verses of "Old Shep", and her howls, combined with Orville's caterwauling, regularly distracted Blue Jay from his writing. Even Messy Bessie joined in. Although she doggedly refused to repeat any English or German words, she learned to imitate Lenore's various barks with a precision that fooled even Blue Jay.

In communicating with her humans, Lenore had developed special vocalizations: There was the urgent whine: "Take me outside immediately. Nature calls;" the plaintive whine: "Pet me. Now. Everyone in this household neglects animals;" the exuberant yelp: "Someone is at the door and I can't wait to jump up and give this person a kiss!" Now, thanks to the addition of Orville's music seeping through the ceiling, dog and bird developed a low, incessant moan, interspersed with an occasional crescendo of yips.

ORVILLE SEEMED to reach his peak cathartic virtuoso performances in late afternoon, during Blue Jay's watch of The Hatchling. Fortunately, most of the tenants were out and about during this time. Only Mrs. Davis's partial deafness spared her from the blast.

Unlike his parents who put forth an aura of friendly extroversion, Travis Grimes was sullen and withdrawn. "Perhaps you'd like to come down and amuse Baby Josh for us or take Lenore on a walk around the block now and then," Lily offered. "It could be a little part-time job for you. Would you like that? I could pay you, like a real job."

"Maybe," he muttered, looking at his shoes.

"Our son has plenty to do up here," Orville interjected. "He's on punishment right now for his sassy mouth."

"Maybe some other time," Lily attempted to soften the blow as a look of hostility flashed across Travis's face.

The true nature of familial relations in the Grimes household revealed itself late in February. True to the predictions in *The Farmer's Almanac*, there was a grand February thaw. Unfortunately, the front stairway carpet had been tracked with dirt from salt and sand carried in on people's boots. Once again, it fell upon Lily to vacuum the stairs and front hall, since Blue Jay had faithfully shoveled and scraped for most of the winter. He offered to take The Hatchling on an outing down the street to visit Ernie and Klara while Lily vacuumed. He had some questions about repairing a leaky faucet in the laundry room, and it would give Lily a time to work without interruption.

Lily discovered that she found comfort in the predictability of building maintenance. Unlike the academic world, these chores were concrete. One could look at a carpet, for example, and say, "This part is done. I have cleaned it; I vacuum very well, for a human-woman. I give myself an A+;" then, turning the other way, one could observe the dirt and say, "This part I now will clean."

She sighed, adjusting the vacuum's brush height. For a belated Christmas gift, Mr. Dreschler had "given" them a new vacuum cleaner and a Christmas handshake. Although she might have preferred a nice box of chocolates or even a big hunk of Cheddar cheese, Lily had marveled over the arrival of the vacuum cleaner as though it had been her heart's desire.

As she vacuumed, Lily thought back over the occasion. It had been an early January morning. Blue Jay had been at the UWM library, so she was left to be the hostess and pose as *caretaker extraordinaire*.

In a moment of inspiration, Lily decided to offer Mr. Dreschler a cup of coffee; in an unguarded moment of response, Mr. Dreschler accepted. Lily took out the delicately painted porcelain cups she had bought at the Goodwill last fall, pleased for the opportunity to use them. Unfortunately, just as Mr. Dreschler was lifting the steaming coffee to his lips, the handle broke off with a little pinging sound, spilling the rich brown liquid all over his neatly pressed silk suit and boiled wool car coat.

"Oh, no!" Lily blurted out. "I am so sorry!" Full of apologies, Lily could not quit talking. She first grabbed a dish towel, then went for a bath towel, seeing that a mere dish towel was an inadequate response.

Mr. Dreschler grabbed the towel and stood up, dabbing at his trousers, which had taken the brunt of the coffee. "This is inexcusable. I try to be generous and look what happens."

He rose to leave. "I will be presenting you with the dry-cleaning bill."

"Oh, but of course!"

Lily first had felt dismay at his abrupt departure, but a moment later she saw the humor of the situation and burst out laughing. "Larry and Lenny will appreciate this!" she gloated. "And I can't wait to tell Jay!"

Her stairwell reverie over this incident was disrupted by a sudden commotion in Apartment 2. The door opened and Sherl ran out, Orville in hot pursuit.

"Omigod!" she said. "What's wrong?"

Sherl was in tears. "I need some ice for my jaw!"

Lily glared at Orville, whose lanky frame now filled the doorway. "What's this about?"

"It's about us. Not your damned business," he snapped.

Turning her back to him, she shoved the vacuum into the corner landing between the first and second floors and said, "I have ice. Sherl, let's go downstairs. Where's Travis?"

"He's at Cub Scouts," she said, and both women exited the building and went around to the back and down the cement stairs to the entrance of the English Basement caretaker's apartment. Orville did not follow.

After wrapping some ice cubes in a towel and pouring a cup of coffee for each of them, Lily asked, "Sherl, why did he do this to you? Does this happen often?"

"I think I broke my jaw," she said. "I—I just fell. He didn't do anything."

Silence filled the kitchen.

"Are you sure?" Lily questioned. "It sounded like more than that was going on."

Another silence, then tears.

Lily ran for a box of tissues, astonished at the sudden turn of events. She went to the door to make sure it was locked, afraid Orville would turn up at any minute. She had sensed something was wrong in this relationship from their first meeting, but the physical violence was a more serious matter than she had suspected.

"He always wants me to serve a fancy breakfast and I was tired. I worked so late last night. Waitressing is hard work, always on your feet, always trying to think ahead about what the customer wants. Working for the tip. Smiling. Frenchy makes all the waitresses wear high heels. My feet ached bad. And he wanted me to get up and cook him salt cod for breakfast. Fish!"

Lily nodded sympathetically, feeling concerned, but outraged at the same time.

"I usually go along with whatever he wants, 'cause he has this mean streak, but today—I don't know—I just couldn't do it."

She dissolved into tears again and Lily ran to get a roll of toilet paper, since they were out of tissues. "All my teeth hurt." She blew her nose so loudly that Messy Bessie became intrigued by the new sound and broke out into a chatter. Ordinarily this would have provoked a laugh from Lily, but instead she threw a dish towel over the cage to silence her. "In the course of only an hour, Sherl has become a friend in need of help." The thought simmered in Lily's mind.

"He always likes fish or fried bacon or something special to eat in the morning. It gets worse in the winter when he's out of work."

"Best you talk about it, Sherl," Lily said, giving her a gentle pat on the shoulder. "It won't go past me."

Sherl looked at the coffee in front of her, paused, and took a deep drink.

Lily sat in silence, hoping that Orville would not see fit to come downstairs and pound on the door, creating more trouble.

Sherl's words gushed out in a torrent.

"My daddy warned me about Orville, but I was too much of a small-town rebel to listen. I got married at age sixteen. You can do that down home.

"'He's pure talent, Daddy,' I'd say. 'You've heard him sing. Orville's gonna be famous one day.' And he'd tell me back, 'He's a good-for-nothing juvenile delinquent. He's just eighteen and already has a record for stealing a car and breaking-and-entering. And even when he was in grade school, he was with some hoods that broke into the school and sprayed obscenities on the walls. A real JD. If you go off with him, don't never think of comin' back.'

"But did I listen? No, first chance I got, the week after I turned sixteen, we eloped.

"You can get married in Mississippi when you're sixteen. Not like up here. Got married by a justice of the peace in Memphis.

"First he treated me like a queen and we had a great time living in motels and traveling around 'til the money ran out. The next thing you know, we're waiting for Travis to get here and Orville is taking day jobs. I ended up with a waitress job."

Lily felt overwhelmed but told herself that sometimes the best you can do is be a good listener. Perhaps Sherl hadn't really been able to talk about this before.

"The first time he beat on me, I was pregnant. I didn't know who to tell and I couldn't go home. Then I figured out how to stop him, just by going along with everything he wanted and being sure that I didn't even so much as glance at another man. I'm real used to waiting on him hand and foot. But you know, like today, sometimes the body just says, 'No. Not now. My bones are weary.'"

"Does the body ever say, 'Enough?' I'd think there would come a point...." Lily's voice trailed off. She hesitated. "If anyone ever treated me like that, I would leave so fast...."

"Well, you know, when I go back upstairs, he'll be real sweet, like nothing ever happened," she broke off. "But one of these times, if he pushes me too far, I will split. I've been stashing away a part of my tips because I won't ever really leave without Travis. Orville bullies Travis, but he don't smack him very often."

She sighed. "I'd hate to think what would happen if I wasn't around. I have to cover for the kid a lot. Travis has a real mind of his own, too."

Sherl pushed back the chair and stood up to leave. "Can I bring this ice pack back later? Speaking of Travis, he should be comin' home soon and I wanna be there. Nothing seems broken and I'm not hurting so much anymore."

"Sure."

"And...thanks.... And please, could we keep all this between us?"

Lily shrugged, "As long as you promise to come down here or call the police if he tries to hurt you again."

"Agreed."

"And one more thing. This building really isn't that soundproof, you know. Our ceiling is your floor. If it's really bad and I hear you calling for help, or I hear you in any trouble at all overhead, I will not hesitate to call the police myself next time. Just so you know." Lily sounded more self-assured than she felt.

"Well, okay, I guess."

A caretaker has to take care of her tenants, you know," Lily smiled, giving her a quick hug. "I am here for you."

And they both went outside and around to the front of the building. For a fleeting moment, Lily worried that Mr. Dreschler's prized vacuum cleaner might have been stolen and she'd have to replace it but found it on the landing just where she had abandoned it. With a sigh, Lily resumed her vacuuming and Sherl disappeared into the depths of Apartment 2.

CHAPTER 7
MARCH

Wherein Lily hosts a "Collaborative Learning" tea party, the occasion of Spring Break is celebrated with a professional photograph and a trip to the museum, Lily contemplates changing her major, an important letter is written, and more trouble brews in the Grimes apartment.

THE WIND HOWLED OUTSIDE, sleet pounding on the windows. Inside the Mediterranean-blue kitchen, Lily and Blue Jay were having a quiet Sunday supper of beef stew with plenty of carrots and garlic, contemplating the weeks stretching before them.

"Perfect beef stew weather!" Blue Jay commented between mouthfuls. The Hatchling was working on shoving several chunks of mashed carrot into his mouth at once, and Lenore was hovering by the legs of the highchair hoping for tasty morsels.

"These past two months have been rough, but this is getting close to the home stretch. I hope the campus can hold itself together long enough for me to graduate. It's like we don't have an academic community of open exchange anymore. Everything is polarized and I'm here in the middle just trying to hang on and get my diploma. Let's hope that March will be better," Blue Jay observed.

"In like a lion, out like a lamb. You know, Blue Jay, it's rough, but I'm glad it's—us. You know? Us."

He nodded. "The problems we have—we can keep at them. Work with them." He paused. "That's the one thing I've never regretted. Us."

"Well, I have. Plenty of times. But when you think of Orville and Sherl and even Mrs. Hopkinson and her perpetual beau, and all the other couples we know that have screwed up relationships, I think it's amazing we've survived even three years."

"It's our inner gyroscopes. Perseverance. And our hope mechanisms." Jay paused, then laughed. "And the fun and challenge of the journey—choices we made and some that were made for us by circumstance."

"Glad I married such an optimist. Maybe we balance each other out. Maybe we're just too busy to think too much. A promise made; a promise kept. We just keep on driving ourselves down whatever road this is." She sighed. "I hope the car doesn't end up in the ditch."

"If we had a car."

"Do you think we should have taken this caretaking job? It sounded so easy, but it's really a lot of work. A juggling act. It's an emotional drain as well as a time commitment."

"Especially since the Grimeses moved in," Blue Jay added.

"You know, I hate to think of the damage they're doing to Travis, not to mention each other. Sociologically speaking, over half of all marriages end in divorce within ten years, and she married him before she even finished high school."

"Did she ever even finish high school? For whatever it's

worth, I think they both made a big mistake. The guy is a total jerk. She fell for the wrong guy. They seem to bring out the worst in each other. Maybe they should both go home and start over."

"She told me her father cut all ties with her when she married Orville the JD."

"Damaged goods. Maybe it could be like the parable of the Prodigal Son—but she's the Prodigal Daughter and he'll slaughter the fatted calf for her."

The conversation drifted on in this fashion. Plans were made for a spring break outing at the museum for The Hatchling, certainly at the ripe old age of eight months old enough to enjoy the sights.

There was also talk of enrolling him in a play group being started on campus through W.I.T.C.H. An empty classroom had been designated by the university's chancellor and the W.I.T.C.H. group was taking donations of toys and furniture to outfit it. Lily thought that it might work out for a couple mornings a week when she was free to help out with the children. Blue Jay was less than enthusiastic, thinking that their little one was still too young to be anywhere without one of them. Lily argued that the other mothers certainly could give emotional support to one another and discuss the challenges of parenting while attending the university. Also, for every hour they volunteered, they could bank an hour of free time for the library or errands. In the back of her mind, Lily still was interested in volunteering at the Underground Switchboard.

Jay was adamant. "He shouldn't be in anyone else's care until he is old enough to tell us about it." The conversation drifted on, issues unresolved.

On this particular evening, no tenants interrupted. The Hatchling fell asleep as if on cue, Messy Bessie's cage was draped, and Lost Lenore was given a quick constitutional. Blue Jay and Lily tumbled into each other's arms.

THE DAYS FLEW by without too many lost keys at Tannenbaum Arms. Campus disruptions had become second nature, and students trudged to class under the dismal shadow of war. On Friday the 13th, Lily and the Hatchling entertained her friend Pam and Pam's tiny daughter Molly with a tea party. Pam and Lily first had met at the well-baby clinic almost a year ago, and now Pam had turned up in Lily's Sociology of Deviant Behavior class.

They had chosen to be partners for a class project and had decided to look at autism. Pam had read a book on the subject. According to Dr. Bruno Bettleheim, a lack of ability to empathize with other humans actually was caused by the mother's lack of bonding with her infant. He had developed a theory of "the refrigerator mother."

The professor believed in collaborative learning, so instead of lecturing, most of the periods were filled with student presentations followed by student-led discussion. "Lily, I'm intrigued by the idea of poor interaction between mother and child, but there seems to be some male chauvinism at work here. Why blame the mother? We could get a good discussion going here, I think."

"Did you ever meet anyone with an autistic child? It would be great to observe interactions first-hand," Lily offered.

"Not really, but I could ask around. This sort of overlaps with my Child Development class. Maybe someone there could help out."

There was a pause as Lily arranged several graham crackers

with cream cheese on a plastic plate for the children and poured apple juice into plastic sipping cups.

"Look what you did, Lily," Pam remarked. "You just gave the blue cup to Little Jay and the pink one to Molly."

"So, what does that mean? I'm burdening the next generation with sexist branding?"

"Probably nothing. Just an observation. Something to think about," Pam replied.

"Next time I'll buy rainbow-colored cups. You know, Pam, you raise a point. It's interesting how you can only find certain clothing items that are good for both girls and boys. They're usually pale yellow or pale green for baby layettes, with little duckies or puppies. It starts that early. You can't put a boy in flowers and ruffles or people look at the parents like they are turning their little boy into a homosexual."

"The Victorians kept their boys in dresses until they could climb trees."

Lily laughed. "I can't imagine The Hatchling in a dress."

"But soon enough he'll be climbing trees. Look at him trying to walk." She paused. "My mom and dad raised me as a frilly girl," Pam continued. "They had three boys and they gave up on ever having a daughter. Then ten years later I came along, a little surprise package. So you see, they treated me like I was a little princess. Overprotected. Pampered. Doted upon. Spoiled rotten, you might say."

Lily nodded. "So, look at you know. You turned out fine. Life seems to bring its corrective lessons," Lily thought ruefully of her own parents—her deceased father, her emotionally absent mother. "I'm just the opposite. The oldest. The built-in babysitter. More Cinderella than princess. But you know, after a while, it doesn't matter as much. You have to move on. I did, and I assume you did, too. Here we are, both sitting here with our schoolwork and our babies, both wearing tie-dyed t-shirts and blue jeans. Smiling. Conversing. Drinking our Constant Comment tea, constantly commenting. I suppose someday these two little ones will look back on us and think of everything we did wrong."

"Or right," Pam interjected. "Think positive."

"Yes, that, too. Maybe," Lily continued.

"Well, at least nobody can accuse us of being refrigerator mothers," Pam said, grabbing Molly in a big squeeze.

The Hatchling lost interest in the tea party, and with his newfound leg strength, swaggered off into the living room. After a few faltering steps, he resorted to crawling at breakneck speed. Molly and Lenore followed at a respectful distance.

Lily sighed, "Well, let's scuttle along and see what mischief they'll find."

The Hatchling headed right to his toy box and pulled out his tambourine. Molly immediately grabbed it and both children began fussing, neither willing to let it go.

"Distraction works best with her," Pam laughed. She reached into the toy box and dangled a sock monkey in front of Molly, who immediately let go of the tambourine and clutched the monkey. "*Dr. Spock's Baby Book* is my guide. Kids this young are really too young to understand sharing, so your best bet is distraction."

"So, any thoughts on being an education major?"

"Yes. It's not such a bad choice for a parent. Generally, you get the same vacations your children have, and summers off for camping and such. And, actually, I find the minds of children are quite amazing. It's like seeing the development of the human race all over again, from the ground up, literally. I like the little people." She looked at Lily. "You should think about getting certified to teach."

Lily had considered herself a devoted scholar, loving nothing better than delving into a good research project, but she realized that she was at a turning point in her academic career. "I should keep my options open. I thought I was on a straight academic track, but now I'm questioning it. And you're right about children. I remember from the moment The Hatchling was born, he was his own person. Looks a lot like a miniature Blue Jay, but really has his own independent soul."

"And by the way, Lily, I probably have no business bringing this up, but now that he's getting older, don't you think maybe he's not a hatchling anymore? He's well-hatched." She smiled, and so did Lily. "Maybe it's time to drop the Hatchling business."

"I think you're right about that. I'm good at cruising on automatic pilot. We call him Little Jay sometimes. I'll think about this. It's amazing, how fast babies grow. A teacher. Hmm."

They agreed to independently research theories of autism and meet after class the following week to outline the presentation, which was not due until the second week in May. Pam left with the observation, "Cold-hearted women, not loving their children? Turning them into isolated little souls? I don't think so. Why do mothers always get such a bad rap? I think I'll try to find some other theories about autism to counter Bettleheim."

The Hatchling fell asleep when the tea party was over. Blue Jay had not yet come home, so Lily sat down at their desk and contemplated the shoes and pant-legs of people passing on the sidewalk, staring blankly through the front windows of their English Basement apartment. Finally, she wrote:

Dear Mom,

It's been a while since I heard from you. I hope everything is okay in Tulsa. Marcus and Missy must be in their terrible

teens by now. I hope they're not giving you too much grief like I know I did.

Since your grandson Little Jay is already nine months old, I thought I would update you on our lives. Joshua and I are both still in school. He is hoping to graduate in June if the campus doesn't explode and I am still plugging away on my master's degree. I am thinking of changing my major from Sociology to Education. I've discovered that the university system is very sexist and I'd rather be part of the change than play their game. (Ha, you're probably saying, "She hasn't changed a bit.") Anyway, we are living rent-free in exchange for managing an apartment building near the university. It's been quite an experience, but not necessarily something I'd ever want to make a career out of. Rent-free applies to the financial aspect only. We pay plenty of "rent" if you count work hours (tending the boiler, shoveling snow, vacuuming carpets) and tenant contact time. I don't know where we'll be next year, but I don't think it will be here. It depends if Joshua gets financial aid for his master's degree somewhere.

Now, to Little Jay. He is the most wonderful miracle I have ever encountered. He has his father's red hair, but our green eyes. He started toddling around last month and his favorite toy is a little tambourine. He is very jolly and not at all shy. He hardly ever cries. He usually jangles his tambourine when he wants to be picked up. Joshua taught him that. He also plays with our dog Lenore, which Josh brought into our marriage with him. That's okay, because I inherited a very noisy, messy parakeet from one of the tenants.

Tulsa seems far away, but it doesn't have to be, really. It would be nice to hear from you sometime. We plan on having Little Jay's picture taken soon. I will send you one, if you like.

I am sending you much love with this letter, Mom. I think about you every day.

Love,
Lily

After writing the letter, Lily sat for a long while, staring out the front window of their English basement, once again watching the feet of the passers-by outside the windows. "I accused Mrs. Grant's daughter of neglect. Maybe I should have been accusing myself. Maybe caring between parents and children has to be more of a two-way street." She debated tearing up the letter and throwing it in the trash, but instead she sealed it in an envelope and wrote the address, not sure it was still where her mother was living.

Later that evening, the phone rang. Expecting a tenant with a complaint, Lily answered with a defensive, "Hello?"

"Lily, it's Pam. I've been thinking. I've been checking things out in the library. I can't find enough on autism to pursue this topic. Just that Bettelheim book that I don't even approve of. I think we should broaden our project to look more generally at varying views on mothering. What do you think?"

"I haven't had a minute to give it another thought. Sure. That's fine with me. It would open it up to interviewing various women of different ages and backgrounds. Could be really interesting." Lily began to see the possibilities. "We could still include a bit about autism, but just not focus on it. Applied sociology. I'd love to work on my interview skills."

They decided to independently develop a list of interview questions and meet after class next week.

On Tuesday evening, good to their word, Larry and Lenny showed up at the door. "Guess what day this is, my friends!"

"Not hard, since you are wearing matching green bow ties,"

Jay laughed. "Come in. You never know who's going to show up here. Maybe a leprechaun will be next."

"We are heading down to Brady Street, but thought we'd stop by here first and share a little Irish cheer." He carried a pitcher. "This is a true shamrock juice cocktail, made in the fabulous Apartment 3 in the famous Tannenbaum Arms by yours truly using only the finest Irish ingredients."

"Always welcome. I have some Irish in me, too. I got my red hair from my Irish grandfather," Jay reached for glasses. "Have a chair."

"In Ireland, there are no snakes, thanks to St. Patrick who drove them all out with a holy rood. And in Chicago, there are probably plenty of snakes, but they've dyed the river green. Although we have a river probably green with pollution, here in Milwaukee the best we can do is drink a little glass of green cheer," Lenny said.

"Or get stumbling drunk," Larry added, "which we're not going to do because tomorrow's a workday."

"Well, didn't you say our Milwaukee Irish all drowned in that Christmas tree ship?" asked Lily.

"Dear, you've got your stories mixed up." Lenny smiled. "Not on the Christmas tree ship. But yes, they drowned that sad night, and Milwaukee never recovered."

"Here's to you! May you be dead a hundred years before the devil knows you're gone!"

Jay and Lily lifted their glasses. The shamrock cocktail was bright green but had a delightful orange flavor on the tongue and burned in the back of the throat, all the way down.

"Cheeers!"

"Maybe it's the luck of the Irish that we have such good neighbors," Jay stated solemnly. "Here's to Tannenbaum Arms!"

• • •

It turned out to be a week of surprises with visitors bearing gifts. Orville and Sherl showed up at their door unexpectedly Sunday afternoon. Sherl carried a plate of *petits fours* and Orville had a large guitar case.

Lily and Jay exchanged quizzical glances, Jay suppressing a laugh at the sight of the guitar case.

"We're just here for a little social call," Orville announced. "How've you been?"

"Come on in, guys," Jay said, restraining Lost Lenore and stepping aside so the twosome could enter.

"I brought you this treat," Sherl smiled. "Left over from work last night. Petty furs. A real French delicacy. Frenchy lets us take leftovers home sometimes."

Jay directed them to seats around the kitchen table. "Please take a chair. Can I get you a cup of coffee?"

Lily looked closely at Sherl and noticed a puffiness and bruise on the lower left side of her face which Sherl obviously had attempted to cover with makeup. "Where's Travis?"

"He's at a friend's house. They're doing homework. Or they better be," was Sherl's reply.

There was a silence.

"Coffee would be great."

"How is work going?"

"Okay. There's this old man, about in his seventies, I think. A fancy dresser with a bow tie and white shirt. He comes for supper every time I work. He always wants to sit in my area. I always give him a big smile, and he always gives me a big tip. Left me a twenty last night!"

Orville frowned.

"I'm not above a little harmless flirtation. I think he's a widower or maybe has a sick wife at home. He wears a flashy diamond on his left hand, but he never has nobody with him. I've been making good tips," she beamed.

"And I have a gig coming up in a couple weeks for a bar mitzvah out in Wauwatosa. They saw my ad in the *Kaleidoscope*. Elvis at a bar mitzvah for a Jewish kid! Shows their good taste. Been practicing. But I guess you've heard me."

Jay laughed. "It would be hard *not* to hear you. It almost never bothers me unless I'm working on memorizing verb tenses in German."

"Would you like a tune?"

Lily put the petits fours on a plate and poured coffee in assorted mugs. "Cream? Or should I ask, 'Skim milk?'"

"A tune?" he repeated.

"Well, sure," Jay agreed, reaching for a *petite four*.

Orville proceeded to take out the guitar and strummed wildly, then broke into a room-blasting version of "All Shook Up."

A cacophony of dissonance followed, as Messy Bessie let forth rhythmic percussive sound and Lost Lenore took up howling. Little Jay looked from one to the other and burst out with his bear growls. Jay and Lily looked at each other in bewilderment and tried not to burst out laughing.

After the song, Jay and Lily politely clapped. "Bravo, Orville! That was...a blast! I'm sure the bar mitzvah lad will be all shook up when you bring this on."

"It's really better when I stand and do the hip motions. Are you ready for an encore?"

"Um, I think I'd better get back to my homework. German verbs are doing me in. Maybe some other time."

"Well," Orville said. "There is one other thing." His voice trailed off.

Sherl fidgeted with her coffee cup, swirling the remains around.

Orville swooped in for the last *petite four*, then leaned back in his chair. "Would it be possible that you could loan us a couple hundred, just for a week or so until a check comes in?"

Jay and Lily exchanged incredulous glances. "Orville, do you realize that we are both students? Sorry. We don't have any money to spare," Jay spoke with an unusual softness in his voice.

Lily thought about adding, "and if we did, we wouldn't want to lend it to you because I don't think we'd ever see it again;" but held her tongue.

He sighed, returning the guitar to its case. "Well, just thought I'd ask."

They made an abrupt exit.

"Well, we found out the real reason for that visit," Jay remarked.

~

Spring Break started on a Wednesday. Liberated from classes, Blue Jay and Lily planned a trip to the photographer along with the museum excursion. Since Lily had thought about sending photographs to Jay's parents and her mother, she thought it might be nice to get a professional photo. Little Jay, formerly known as The Hatchling, was in fine form, smiling at the world from his vantage point in the back carrier.

He had recently learned to tease Blue Jay by patting him on the head when perching in the back carrier. Blue Jay responded with an exaggerated, "Owww!" which evoked a melodic giggle from Little Jay. Blue Jay loved the sound of his son's laughter, so he kept the game going as they crossed Gertie the Duck's bridge over the Milwaukee River, past Gimbel's, past the Woolworth's —the former home of Messy Bessie—and on down the crowded main street.

The photographer was located on Wisconsin Avenue in the

back of the J.C.Penney's Department Store, just a short distance from the museum, so the whole trip could be accomplished with the Bus 15 to Water Street and a few blocks of walking.

As they passed through the department store aisles, Lily paused, temporarily lured by display counters of thick towels and colorful blankets on sale. The general strategy had been to stay out of such places because of their constrained budget. She sighed. Some plush towels would be nice. But she kept those thoughts to herself.

When they reached the photographer's bailiwick, they were greeted by an array of larger-than-life baby head posters displayed in shades bordering on fluorescent. At first Little Jay was put off by the bald, bespectacled photographer and made a dour face, but when Lily plunked him down on a low stool and took his trusty tambourine out of her purse, he smiled obligingly. The toddler proved to be in an unusually mellow mood and actually seemed to play to the camera. After several flashes and a graham cracker treat, they were ready for the museum. "The proofs will be sent out within a week," the photographer assured them, shifting his bifocals up to his forehead. "I think we got some good ones, although it is a bit unusual to take pictures of a child with a tambourine. He's a very photogenic child."

"I'm sure every parent believes that," Blue Jay said.

They walked down the avenue, savoring the sheer joy of a brisk March day. "Maybe we'll see Gertie the Duck!" Lily exclaimed. She felt exuberantly alive, finally liberated from the heavy boots and wraps of winter.

The large department store windows featured displays of pastel-clad mannequins wearing jaunty hats and frozen smiles; the streets were filled with people who seemed to be rushing to important appointments. A few staunch-hearted picketers loitered in front of the Army Recruitment storefront, but it was too early in the day for any important action.

Jay looked longingly in the windows of the Harry Schwartz Bookshop and the Renaissance Book Store, making a note to himself to visit soon. The thought of Little Joshua loose in a bookstore was more than he could contemplate.

They arrived at the museum entrance at 10:00 A.M. just as it was opening. They checked in their coats and the back carrier and splurged on the rental of a bright-yellow duck-shaped museum stroller.

"Where to first, Lily?" Blue Jay asked.

"Let's start with the dinosaurs here on the first floor and then just work our way up to the second floor."

"Agreed."

They proceeded through the portal, a tunnel-like cave with large plastic stalactites and stalagmites and emerged in a prehistoric world filled with great dioramas of monsters created from the intersection of science and dreams—the flamboyant *stegosaurus*, the snarling *tyrannosaurus rex*, and the wistful mastodon. Instead of showing fear, Little Jay excitedly kicked his feet and tried to crawl out of the stroller so he could join these animals.

"He must think they're just some big green puppies," Blue Jay remarked.

"Look, Little Jay! *Pterodactyl*!" Lily attempted to distract him from the great primordial pampas scene. "Let's push on, Jay," she said.

The next stop was the Native American display at the top of the second floor. There was a gigantic diorama of Sioux Indians on a buffalo hunt, complete with life-sized buffalo and thundering sound effects.

"This is a very accurate scene in every detail, even the moccasins," Blue Jay observed. "Of course, the indigenous people had a cyclic concept of time—not like our linear outlook. They killed these buffalo by corralling the herd and driving it over a cliff. They used the skin, the bones, the meat—everything for survival. But they believed that the cyclical nature of the world would cause these buffalo to be reborn in the Spring."

"I see I'm a captive audience for a lecture," Lily said. "Just wait until Little Jay is a bit bigger. Maybe in a couple years."

Blue Jay shrugged. "Well, at least we can show him the Milwaukee dwellers' secret."

"Sure."

"Tourists never get this and we don't tell! Local pride, you know."

They went over to a rock on the far right-hand side of the diorama. Jay bent down and pressed a door-bell-like button hidden behind the rock. A coiled rattlesnake twitched its tail and gave its rattled warning whenever the button was pushed.

"Look, Little Jay," Lily said. "Snake! See the snake!"

Blue Jay lifted him out of the stroller and guided his finger to push the button.

"Da!" he said. "Da!"

"Say snake, Little Jay!"

"Da!" Little Jay replied, looking very proud of himself as he tried to push the button on his own.

"I think he's telling us that he understands cause and effect," observed Lily. "You push the button, the snake shakes his rattle."

They moved on through the Native American exhibit, pausing by the skeleton familiarly known to regular museum-goers as the Aztalan princess, with her elaborate stone necklace draped around her neck vertebrae and over her now-exposed ribs.

"She's beautiful even now, Blue Jay," Lily whispered. "I always visit her whenever I come to the museum."

"Yes, but this hurts me. We've got to get these bones out of here. How would you feel if a thousand years from now people came and stared at your bones?"

Lily laughed, "Well, I'm sure it wouldn't matter to me at that point, would it?"

"I don't find this amusing," Blue Jay asserted. "I find this is a violation of humane treatment of a corpse. The Aztalan people were not indigenous to Southern Wisconsin. No one knows where they really came from or how they disappeared. Some people think they are related to the Aztecs, but that's been disproved. Over by Lake Mills you can visit the remains of one of their wooden fortresses. They were mound builders. Their mounds are all around that area." He walked over to another display, a small reconstruction of the Aztalan village. "Look. This shows how they stuck these poles up in a huge circle to protect their community of separate lodges."

"Blue Jay. Stop. You're lecturing me again. I don't need it." Then, to soften her words she added, "It's just—I'm a separate person. I need to experience this in my own way. Let's visit Aztalan sometime," Lily said.

"It's about halfway between here and Madison. Maybe this summer we can get there," Blue Jay agreed. "Anyway, there is a strong movement by Native American groups to remove all ancestral bones from museums, and also to return precious artifacts to the descendants or to tribal custody."

"But some of this stuff, it's good to see firsthand," Lily argued. "Most people are not without empathy, you know."

"When we first got our television set in the late fifties there was a television Indian on a children's show called *Howdy Doody*, who used to say, 'Ugh! Me Big Chief Thunderthud. Kill many buffalo. Hear my war cry,' and then he'd make a twisted little yodel sound. I don't think of it every day, but somewhere that's stuck in the back of my brain like a tape-recorded message. How many thousands of people still have this little message and others like it whirling around in their brain cells? This all needs to be worked out," Blue Jay mused. "It really calls for a more respectful outlook, I think."

"Well, I'll sign a statement now," Lily persisted. "To Whom It May Concern in Future Centuries: You have permission to put my bones on display if it will further the understanding and appreciation of the typical Wisconsin citizen in the Year of Our Lord, 1970."

"Rest in peace, Princess of Aztalan," Blue Jay muttered.

They moved on in silence, looking at the various reconstructed Woodland Native American habitats. "I can't wait for our trip to the Upper Peninsula this summer," Blue Jay burst out. "I have a lot of favorite places—including Ojibwa home sites. I even figured out where my ancestor, Chief Andrew J. Blackbird, used to live. A beautiful view of Lake Superior is about all that's left."

"Once a Yooper, always a Yooper," Lily responded. "Why is my world filled with Yippies and Yoopers?" She laughed. "Seriously, though, I'm looking forward to the visit." She wheeled the duck stroller through a portal defined by four pseudo-Corinthian pillars. "Let's go peek into the Ancient Civilizations Wing before Little Jay or I have a meltdown. The Minoan stuff is my other favorite. I'll pretend I'm back in Crete. No bones there, just coins and pottery shards and an amazing snake goddess figurine. Archaeologists call her *Potnia*, but if no one has cracked the Minoan language, I don't know how they figured out that was her name."

Lily was spellbound by the shards and statuary in this case and could have stayed there longer. "These pieces are all stories, just waiting to be perceived," she speculated. "It's a journey into the past that gives us understanding of ourselves."

Little Jay was growing weary of sitting in the duck stroller and his naptime was approaching, so after a quick visit to the Minoan display and an even quicker walk-through of the Pre-Columbian Room, they decided to leave. "You can't do it all in one day," Blue Jay observed.

"Especially with a toddler," Lily agreed.

Little Jay fell asleep in his back carrier on the bus and snuggled against his father's shoulder snoring lightly. By the time they got home, Lily and Blue Jay were ready for a nap, but Little Jay had a second wind and Lenore was ecstatic and in need of a constitutional.

The other highlight of the day of the museum visit was a special dessert. Lily had made apple cake the night before. Little Jay made a total mess of it and ended up with the sticky cream cheese frosting on his nose and in his hair and all over his little sailor suit which he had been dressed in for the picture. She sighed. The outfit had remained remarkably clean, up to this point.

"Time for a splish-splash, Little Jay," Blue Jay said, scooping him out of his highchair and flying him like a model airplane into the bathroom. "Let's go find Gertie, your rubber duckie."

"Just last year at this time I was a blimp," thought Lily. "A six-months-pregnant blimp trying to hide her blimpiness under big sweaters to keep her research assistantship. Now look at this Wonder Child. A child really teaches the parent a big lesson about love. And also a lot about expanding and contracting." She smiled as he splashed in the tub, then ran around the kitchen naked as a blue jay as she cleared away the cake crumbs and washed down the highchair tray.

WITH SPRING IN THE AIR, the feeling of confinement gave way to a strange combination of desperation and euphoria. The tenants in Apartment 6 began to invite large numbers of friends over for almost nightly jam sessions. They used their acquired mimeograph machine and began printing brief updates and background articles on protest activities in the university area.

"These could be historic documents," Jay mused, as he found a copy of the latest bulletin that Bob had placed in their doorway. He went for the coffee pot and poured himself a cup, not bothering to re-heat it. He plopped down into a chair and held out the paper to Lily. "Here's useful information. Look at this. They're starting a Free University. All sorts of person-to-person classes. I could teach a poetry workshop for them. Well, not now, but maybe later once I'm done with the semester."

Lily took a more practical approach. "We have to check the front hall so they don't decide to post it and get us fired."

"And this is good to know, Lily. There are several narcs out there, sitting in on our classes, pretending to be part of the revolution, but actually they are spying on us and our professors. This gives their names."

"So we can assume they will soon be job hunting," Lily laughed.

"Lily, don't make light of this. The thought that anyone next to you is a rat-fink spreads a feeling of distrust and alienation across the campus." He paused. "You know, this will all be history someday. All done, all gone. I wonder how many people like that Marquette dude I met are out there collecting things like this hand-out. These papers are artifacts, really."

"Every age has its own issues."

"But these are our issues, and this is our time. I think we are really part of a great revolution."

"Maybe every generation feels like that. Our parents had World War II and Korea and their parents had the Great Depression." Lily scowled, not in the mood for this conversation.

"But maybe some people in the future will care. Will want

to hear about this. Maybe some future Hatchling of the Hatchling."

Lily looked at him solemnly. "Like Dylan says, 'The country I come from is called the Midwest.' He nailed that all right. I sometimes think we are just little Midwestern people that nobody outside our little world gives a damn about; so we have to care about ourselves and each other. We are Riesman's Lonely Crowd. Maybe we will all have to go around with invisible shields to protect us from narcs and smoke bombs." Lily was getting into her own thoughts, which could make Jay uneasy if she continued in that direction too long.

"Jay, we have this little world that we live in. English Basement Cocoon World. Tannenbaum World. UWM World, all impacted by Outside World. Most people I know don't give up trying to make things better. We fight back against injustice in our own fashion. Is this how a revolution looks from the bottom up?"

Jay tried to pull her back with humor. It usually worked when Lily started to descend into one of her angry "Poor Lily" moods. "Bottoms up!" he said, tepid coffee cup in hand.

She scowled as he grabbed a poem out of the air. "As the great Emily Dickinson once said, *I'm nobody; Who are you? Are you nobody, too?*"

His strategy worked. She laughed.

"Blue Jay, I usually don't know your poets, but I happen to know that one from high school. She's an old-timer. Never trust anybody over a hundred and thirty. I don't have to worry about being 'public like a frog.' I suppose you'll have to teach that one to Little Jay. I wonder if they still teach that poem to high schoolers."

Jay shook his head, pulling another quote out of his endless supply. "These are the times that try men's souls...." He fingered the mimeographed sheet and re-read it, then carefully placed it in a manila folder where he kept special papers. "Someday I might want to look at this and remember...."

Bongo Bob from Apartment 6 moved to Madison where he felt he would be closer to the real action and was replaced by Jeff Somebody from Madison who felt ready for a new scene. According to Dan, Jeff had been over-involved in the Madison protests and wanted to be more anonymous. Blue Jay and Lily maintained an attitude of benign neglect; as long as none of the other tenants complained. As long as the "Sixers", as they were privately nicknamed, refrained from clogging drains with candle wax or filling the main stairwell with marijuana fumes, or posting their mimeographed fliers in the front hall, the caretakers chose not to intervene. The revolving band of tenants in Apartment 6 always were conscientious about turning over the rent, so Mr. Dreschler didn't complain either.

March had come in like a lion, had a lamb-like middle, and morphed again for a lion's exit, as well. Spring retreated and everyone searched for misplaced mittens as a thick snow swirled around them. The citywide schools were cancelled for the day, buses immobilized. "This is the perfect day for long-simmered home-made chili," Lily declared, searching in the pantry for a can of beans.

"A snowstorm in March does not have the same impact as a blizzard in December or January," Blue Jay remarked to Lily as he pulled on his boots to shovel the sidewalk. "Even as you push the dang white stuff one more time, you realize that the earth is tilting on its axis and soon it will be Spring. If we weren't the caretakers, I'd just let the snow sit there until the sun did its job."

As he was about to leave the apartment to shovel, the phone rang. "I'll get it. Go ahead," Lily said.

It was Mrs. Davis. "I think you'd better come upstairs. There's something strange going on with those new tenants in Mrs. Grant's old apartment."

CHAPTER 8

APRIL

Wherein the Grimeses become the center of an April Fool's Day mystery, Blue Jay's reputation as a *poet of note* grows, the city celebrates Earth Day at the edge of Lake Michigan, Lily receives an important letter, and the caretakers are called upon to perform a heroic rescue.

INDEED, Mrs. Davis had been correct. There was some strange business going on in Apartment 2. After receiving Mrs. Davis's phone call, Blue Jay dashed across the still-unshoveled slushy sidewalk to the front of the building.

"April Fool's joke, I hope."

Lily followed, grabbing Little Jay and carrying him in what she called the "flour sack" hold—unceremoniously tucked under her arm, balanced on a slightly jutted hip. When they reached the front door of Apartment 2, they found it hanging open. No lights were on; once again Apartment 2 held the stillness of a tomb. Fearing the worst, Lily softly called, "Sherl!"

No answer; only the deceptive serenity of a snowy Saturday with the occasional clank and hiss of a radiator.

They stepped inside. "Sherl!"

Blue Jay flicked on the foyer light. They walked through the hall, cautiously peering into each room. Lily attempted to make a joke. "Hey, Ned Nickerson, now I know how Nancy Drew felt."

The kitchen was at the rear of the apartment, adjacent to the fire escape. The entire apartment was empty, except for a sinkful of smashed, dirty dishes, including a sticky frying pan that smelt of bacon and fish.

"Yuk! Well, goodbye, Grimeses!" Blue Jay sighed. He turned to Lily. "Not even a note or a thank you. Mr. Dreschler's gonna love this."

"I just hope Sherl is okay. I wonder if she showed up for work at Frenchy's last night or if they split town."

"And that poor kid. No wonder he was so moody if this is the life he leads," Blue Jay shook his head. "Well, I guess I'd better shovel the snow. Nothing like a little physical labor to blunt an emotional trauma."

"So I get to call Mr. Dreschler?"

"I thought you'd never ask. Ned Nickerson often left such tasks to Nancy Drew, the number one lady detective role model."

"No. Drop the Nancy business. Just call me Lily, the Vacuum Cleaner Lady. Suck it up. I don't think they swept or dusted since they moved in."

"Well, what do you expect from someone named Grimes?"

They stood amidst the dust bunnies and laughed until tears came. The bad pun brought comic relief. Even Little Jay joined in the laughter, although he didn't know why.

News of Blue Jay's upcoming publication in the prestigious literary magazine *Undercurrents* spread around the English Department. He was invited to read for Professor Wright's freshman honors English class where he was greeted with near celebrity status. After reading several poems, students plied him with questions. "When did you start writing?" and "How long does it take to write a poem?" and "Where do you get your inspiration?" all seemed startlingly simple to him; but he realized the genuineness behind the questions and answered them all with patience and respect.

"How long does it take to write a poem?" seemed to be a good place to start.

"Some nights, maybe an hour for a two-liner..." Jay paused. "Or an image or some words might just pop into my head at any time, day or night, and I will take out my trusty notebook and jot them down." He reached into his jacket pocket and pulled out a small legal pad, filled in with very small cursive. "Here's show-and-tell."

He replaced it. "Of course, later on I will sit alone with the words and maybe something will emerge that I want to keep. But like everything else, poetry is part inspiration and skill and part discipline. It is a demanding taskmaster. You need to listen to its call and dedicate yourself to keeping the mindset alive."

Receiving a nod of encouragement from Professor Wright, Jay continued. He got a laugh from the group when he revealed that he recommended hugging trees and confessed that he had a favorite oak tree in Riverside Park; but received several blank stares when he told them that he read Goethe and Dylan Thomas. He also recommended the musical poetry and poetic music of Leonard Cohen and Bob Dylan, proclaiming them two of the greatest sages of the age.

After class, Professor Wright shook Blue Jay's hand and offered to give him a strong letter of recommendation to include with his graduate school applications. "You are planning to go on, aren't you?" He was an older, gray-haired man with a lifetime of researching and teaching behind him. He reminded Jay of the stereotypical English professor in worn tweedy jacket with leather elbow patches and bifocals perched halfway down his nose. He had published an anthology of American Literature that was still in wide use, although a group of Native Americans in Minnesota had challenged some of his choices of selections for inclusion. "But Mr. Haakens, you should think about applying for a teaching assistantship right here at UWM. We're developing a graduate program in English and you could be in on the ground floor. We plan to have some reciprocity with UW Madison. Credits would be accepted here, and you could take the Badger Bus to Madison a couple times a week for some advanced work, in case you saw something intriguing. You could use the bus ride for study time. I would surely put in a good word for you."

Blue Jay left Bolton Hall smiling, more confidence in his step than he had felt for a long time. Maybe, just maybe, things would work out.

Since he had some time to spare, he decided to make his way down the few blocks toward a familiar haunt, the Tuxedo on Downer. The moist lake air held a hint of Spring, as he inhaled deeply. Someone called out his name.

"Blue Jay!"

"Hi, Moisette. Long time, no see. How's life? Everything must be going okay up in Apartment 5. We haven't heard from you lately."

She matched his steps and they proceeded together. "Yes, fine! We're getting another roommate soon, to help out with the rent."

"Oh?"

"Yeah. I plan to travel this summer. My daddy gave me a

round-trip ticket to Paris, so this guy I met will be taking over my room. Just for the summer."

"Well, why don't you bring him down and introduce him?" Blue Jay took the news quite calmly.

"I plan to go to abroad on a self-designed tour which I'm calling 'Moisette's Seven Wonders of Europe.' So far, though I only have six lined up. Maybe I'll stop off in London and visit Windsor Castle. That could be number seven. The queen is really German, you know."

"So, what are the other six?" Blue Jay couldn't resist asking.

"Well, there's the big French cathedral, Notre Dame. That's French for 'Our Lady,' referring to Mary, of course. And probably there can be two wonders in one city since it's Paris. I think I'd like to visit the Eiffel Tower. My daddy took me there when I was about six years old, but I hardly remember, except we got stuck in the elevator. Scary. Then on to Switzerland to see an Alp in person. You know. Stay in a resort on top of those tall mountains where rich people go to ski, even though it won't be the right season. Or will it? Because snow stays on those mountains all year round. I would consider the Alps a wonder."

She paused and looked at Blue Jay. "You know, you'd be a pretty good travel companion. Daddy would probably spring for a ticket for you, too, because he's worried about an attractive girl like me traveling alone."

Blue Jay looked at her incredulously and swallowed a laugh. "Maybe you should take the would-be summer tenant along. Lily and I have plans for the Upper Peninsula the summer. Big plans."

"Groovy," she smiled. "Maybe I'll come back engaged to a duke."

"Well, Moisette, I'm not sure that there are too many loose dukes running around the Alps. He could be your seventh wonder. Good luck, though."

As they approached the Tux, Moisette continued on to the grocery store. "See you back at the Tannenbaum," she said.

"Stay cool!" Blue Jay waved.

"Peace out!"

Inside the Tux, Blue Jay spotted Frank sitting by the window filling a spiral notebook with his spidery writing. He nodded to Eddie the Bartender, and noisily pulled out a chair across from Frank, who finished a sentence and looked up. "Hi, Bro!"

"How about a frothy glass of Schlitz? Treat's on me."

"You buyin'?"

"You bet." He walked to the bar. "Two taps, Eddie. Please."

"Well, ain't you the big spender today!"

Blue Jay smiled. "Gotta treat your friends right."

"And your enemies wrong?" Eddie quipped.

"Actually, killing with kindness would probably be a better strategy. Think Ghandi and King," Blue Jay said as he took the two glasses over to the table.

"What's up, Franko? I hope I'm not interrupting."

"Sure, you're interrupting, but that's okay. I'm just trying to jot down more background for my novel. Calling it *Respite in Hell*, but the name changes just about every week. You just missed Pete. He's planning activities for another event. Talked non-stop. He never quits. An Earth Day reading on Bradford Beach. Later this month. Coming up. I needed a break from my other break." He nodded at the glasses. "And the froth is free to flow."

"Nice alliteration. Did you hear what happened here on campus with the Chicago 7 verdict? Some of the professors joined the students and now their bids for tenure are in question. Including Young Dr. Frankenstein from English."

"Frawwwwnkinschtein. Everything is so political, even teaching."

"Especially teaching. I think the faculty is torn apart. At least they're taking the issues seriously since the Hayakawa debacle."

"You know, Frank, I totally missed that. It was Valentine's Day and I must have been busy with one thing or another at the building. We covered his book, *Language in Action*, in Wiegner's class last year."

"I took that class, too, remember? Dangers of propaganda. A critical attitude toward language. Susceptibility to sloganeering and following tyrants because of their persuasive rhetoric. But he turned from being an academician to a politician. Or propagandist. This night was about politics." He paused. "You missed another scene. The SDS held a protest outside when they couldn't get in."

Jay nodded. "Sometimes the SDS is our conscience, but they don't always know when to quit."

"He deserved that treatment. You gotta know the background from Cali. He turned out to be a little guy with a silver sword of a tongue. He started out as a clever linguist but turned out to be one of the tyrants his own book warned us about. His visit here got a little uncomfortable when the protesters threw smoke bombs into the Union ballroom and pelted the windows with stones. I was sitting in the middle and was afraid I would have an asthma attack, even though I haven't had one since eighth grade."

"The mystery of history. The irony of tyranny," Jay replied. "Not too sad I missed that event."

The door opened, creating a swath of light in the semi-dark interior. Frank waved at the young woman hesitating in the doorway, her hair a glowing halo in the backlight. "Rosie!"

She joined them. "How's the novel going, Frank? Hi, Jaybird!" She reached over and took a sip of Frank's beer.

"What's going on with Poets for Peace? I missed you over at the Gibson's house. Quite a read-in."

"I'm on a brief sabbatical. It's called grad school applications and German irregular verbs," Blue Jay replied. "How about you?"

She hesitated. "I'm not writing, either. In fact, I'm thinking of dropping out of school for a while after this semester. It's like this great bat of despair is blocking out the sun. I can't write and I can't even think straight. I question why I'm even staying in Milwaukee. This bat is hovering and I keep hearing my own voice, but whispering in my ear like waves hitting the shore, again and again, 'Why bother? Why bother? And I hate my apartment now.'"

Frank leaned forward, "What is this about, Rose?"

She broke into tears. "You know Elly? My roommate? I should say, my ex-roommate. You know, she tried to kill herself on St. Patrick's Day night. She never gave a sign. Always cheery like a Chatty Cathy doll. I was out partying and when I came home, I found her in the bathroom with blood all over the floor. She slashed her wrist. I called the police and they sent an ambulance over. First she was out at Bayside Psych, but now they've sent her back to Sheboygan by her parents and they won't even let her friends visit. But the weird thing is I didn't even know anything was that seriously wrong. And now I just can't move on."

Her voice trailed off. "All the while I cleaned her blood off the floor, I was beyond tears. Do you know how thick and messy blood is? It just wouldn't mop up. The more I tried to wipe it, the more it sloshed around. Evil finger paint on the floor. Finally I just took a bucket and dumped it on the tile and then sopped it up with towels and threw all the towels out. I thought Elly and I were close. We talked all the time. I knew about her boyfriend being sent to Vietnam, but I never realized how much she was hurting inside."

"So now you've got a bat in your belfry," Frank prodded. "You. You are not the type to be a bat hostess, Miss Rosie, my friend."

She smiled. "Apparently I am. Just like I thought Elly was not the type to try to take her life."

"I didn't really know her that well. Only met her when you brought her along to the Kinnell reading," Frank continued. "Maybe too much alcohol just got to her. That's a rough time to be alone. Too much green beer and forced cheer and shamrocks sprouting out of nowhere."

"She even seemed contented enough, no more problematic than the rest of us. A couple times she dropped acid, smoked a little hash, but mostly she stayed away from the drug scene," Rosie continued. "She'd check the mailbox a couple times a day, just waiting for letters from her boyfriend. Kept all those letters in an old cedar candy box by her bed. She said he was going through hell over there, dropping napalm on jungles and such, which he wrote her about."

"Well, she wouldn't have been much use to him if she had succeeded in killing herself. I wonder if he knows about this," Blue Jay remarked.

Frank and Rosie both stared at him, as if they had forgotten his presence at the table. Jay laughed nervously. "Well, I guess I'd better be going. It's my turn for Kid Patrol at the Tannenbaum." He stood up and they exchanged their goodbyes. By the time he was out the door, Frank had reached across the table and covered Rosie's hand with his as a gesture of consolation. Their conversation resumed.

~

Blue Jay walked solemnly down Oakland Avenue, contemplating the ups and downs of his tumultuous life as a poet. Lily had taken Little Jay out for a stroller ride and met him as he rounded the corner about a block east of Tannenbaum Arms. When they returned home, there was a letter in the mailbox with a Tulsa postmark and a four-word note taped to their door: ***Call me. Oscar Dreschler***.

"It's your turn to call him, Blue Jay," was Lily's only response as she seized the letter and retreated to the bedroom for privacy. Tears welled up as she recognized her mother's bold script:

Dear Lily,

I received your letter last month and I have thought about what I could possibly say to you. Of course, you are also in my thoughts. Now that you are a parent, you should know that a parent's love never quits. But circumstances here are very tough. I am working part time as a bank teller, just hanging on financially.

I suppose I should have told you about this a long time ago, but I didn't want you to worry. I'm sorry to say that things are not going well with Clem. About four years ago he was diagnosed with a disease called multiple sclerosis, which is gradually getting worse. There is no treatment for it, although we keep hearing about experimental drugs in the offing. Clem can't ride his motorcycle anymore. I didn't have the heart to mention it to him, but finally last month the realization struck him. We went out to the Harley store here in Tulsa and posted his motorcycle for sale on the bulletin board. Finally letting it go was a tough decision. It means that now he is condemned to riding passively in a sidecar at the kindness of his pals. The MS has especially affected his legs and his sense of balance. It seems so cruel to me, that fate should have afflicted him like this, since his greatest pleasure in life was

the freedom of getting on that motorcycle, revving the engine, and taking off for who-knows-where. And any profits from the motorcycle will have to go to pay for the experimental drugs.

As for me, it seems that I never can escape the caretaker's role. Maybe you got that from me. First your father and now Clem. Funny, isn't it? Mother and daughter are both doing some kind of caretaking job. I do hope you will soon be able to move on to better circumstances. I know how demanding this can be—buildings and people. Clem now has an open pressure sore on his foot and I must change these bandages several times a day. I have to load him into a special van equipped with a wheelchair lift. Who knew? When I married him, I thought I was escaping all the pain that I felt after the death of your father, but now after a reprieve of a few years I'm right back into it.

As for your half-brother Marcus, he is following in your footsteps. He left home about a year ago and we occasionally hear from him. As of January when he last called us, he was living in a commune near Hot Springs, Arkansas, doing farm labor. They don't eat any meat and they meditate. Seven times a day, he said. They follow this little fat boy guru. I forget his name. He seems okay, but he's just seventeen now and I wish he'd get it in his head to at least finish high school. I'm thinking that maybe he'd go stay with you for a while in Milwaukee or wherever you'll be next fall and you and Joshua could influence him to go back to school. I could scrape together the cash to send him a bus ticket. Missy doesn't worry me so much. She loves art and spends her spare time filling sketchbooks.

I am glad to hear that my grandson is such a remarkable little boy. I look forward to meeting him some day. I hope you realize that right now I am in over my head with troubles. But I think about you every day and I would like to have one of

those pictures of Little Joshua that you mentioned. I would be proud to put it on my desk at the bank.

I am sending you my love. Greet both Joshuas for me.

Mother

PS: Speaking of pictures, I always kept your father's camera. It is an expensive one, with a German Leica lens. Next to you, it was his dearest treasure. He had a gift for catching just the right moment in a photo. I want you to have it. Maybe you can learn to take your own pictures. Also, there is a manila envelope of pictures he took—some in the Army in Korea and some of you as a toddler. I will be sending them out for you but need to wait until I can find a very safe box for shipping the camera. It's valuable. I almost sold it once, but now I am glad I had second thoughts about that. Check your mail in about a week.

LILY PLACED the letter back in its envelope and stuck it under her pillow. She went back into the kitchen where Blue Jay was engaged in heated conversation with Mr. Dreschler. "No, I didn't hear them leave. They left in the middle of the night. How could I know?" (pause) "No, they didn't give any signs." (pause) "Yes, I know we're the caretakers and we should always be on duty day and night, twenty-four hours a day. Yes, Mr. Dreschler." (pause) "No, we don't drink." (pause) "Yes, we were home. We were asleep." (pause) "I was just heading out to shovel snow when Mrs. Davis called us." (pause) "Yes, we check the front hall. But it was just eight in the morning."

Lily shook her head in disbelief. Mr. Dreschler was blaming them for the unexpected departure of the Grimes family. That seemed so unreasonable. "Blue Jay, tell him to try contacting Sherl at Frenchy's," she whispered.

"Maybe you can contact Mrs. Grimes at Frenchy's," Blue Jay

echoed. “I’m sorry that all the money you ever got was the deposit, but you know we don’t handle the rent. Maybe she still works there.” (pause) “Thanks, Mr. Dreschler. We try.” He hung up the receiver and just stood there in the middle of the kitchen shaking his head. “That man is not reasonable. How can he think this is our fault?”

“Sometimes he just doesn’t get it,” Lily responded. “At least I heard from my mother. You can read it later. It’s a good letter, mostly full of sad news. Except for the end. I’m getting my dad’s camera! I didn’t even know he had one, and now I can’t wait!” She burst into tears.

Two days later, upon Mr. Dreschler’s bidding, Lily and Jay were working in the small, back bathroom of Apartment 2. Papers covered the exquisite hexagonal tiles on the floor and a paint tray was delicately balanced on the toilet.

“Lovely way to spend a rainy day, ya know. Too bad the Grimeses couldn’t have stayed a couple more months and we would have been done with this place.” Jay sighed and dipped his roller into the pale-blue paint.

“Mr. Dreschler is so unreasonable. Like it’s our fault they ditched?”

Little Jay was having a grand time with all the empty space, running from the living room all the way to the butler’s pantry and back again, with little detours into the vacant bedrooms. Since there was no furniture and nothing he could get into as far as they knew, Lily and Jay let him have free range in the apartment while they focused their attention on the bathroom.

“Let’s blitz this. It’s too nice to spend all day like this. We could be walking in the rain or dancing in puddles or...”

Lily burst into a loud, slightly off-key version of “Just a little rain falling on the ground. The grass lifts its head to the heavenly sound."

Just then Jay swerved sharply to block Little Jay as he toddled in at the sound of his mother's singing.

Just as she got to "What have they done to the rain?" the precariously balanced paint tray yielded to the force of gravity and clanked onto the tile floor.

"Dang! Grab the baby!" Lily shouted, since she was on the far side of the tub.

"Too late, Lily!" Little Jay slipped on the floor and slithered down with a splat into the gooey mess.

The toddler burst out into a chuckle, lifting his paint-wet palm to his red curls. Lily moved fast and in one swoop lifted him into the tub and turned on the water. She grabbed his hand just as he was going to suck his gooey blue fingers. "Oh, no, you don't! Tubby time is here! One of these days we'll have to give you your first haircut if you keep this up."

Jay went downstairs for rags and towels to clean up the mess. Little Jay's screams could be heard all the way as he exercised his right to protest a vigorous hair-wash.

"Good thing Mr. Dreschler got cheap latex paint. Good thing toddlers are relatively washable," Lily mused, removing Little Jay from the porcelain torture chamber. The absurdity of the situation was beginning to grab her, and soon all three of them were laughing, although the thought of the extra work was daunting.

Jay was determined to finish the job after cleaning the tile. Lily hustled Little Jay downstairs, depositing his paint-smeared overalls in the trash on her way. Lenore greeted them in the doorway, as always ready for a romp. Lily and Little Jay were ready for a nap.

~

There is always one of those spring days in Milwaukee when one opens the front door to be greeted with a kiss in the face by a velvet-soft breeze. On this day, the sun is so warm that the last vestiges of diminished glaciers retreat to oblivion in their shady corners. On this day, as if part of a great, orchestrated Dance of the Lemmings, the good citizens of Milwaukee forsake all responsibility and head for Lake Michigan. To be living in a city perched on the edge of this Great Lake means constantly to be in touch with edges. The edge of the state, the edge of the lake. The edge of the world, sea meeting sky with a dream of land invisible in the east; each grain of sand on Bradford Beach a cosmos; each bit of fossilized crinoid chain snatched from the place where sand and water meet—a reminder that this is also the edge of time. And Time greets the good citizens and says, "Congratulations, you've survived another Winter. Warm yourself in the sunlight, take off your shoes, leave toe tracks in the sand, then dance to the music of the spheres. It's the springtime of the world."

In the Spring of 1970, this day of wonder coincided with the officially designated "Earth Day," April 22. This first-ever event had been the inspiration of a Wisconsin senator, Gaylord Nelson, who had pushed forth legislation to give it national credence. People called him a tree hugger and pie-eyed optimist; but a nation in poisonous embattlement within and without sorely needed a chance to share a few hugs and shake off the cloak of gloom, however temporarily. The official Earth Day celebration was planned for the Milwaukee River, with its polluted run-offs, with its dead rats floating downstream. Crews of people were doing a clean-up there, ending in a teach-in the downtown area.

On this Earth Day Blue Jay and Lily, along with The Lost Lenore and Little Jay, rose early, ignoring customary activities of attending classes, doing homework and laundry. They joined the crowds already on the lakefront to participate in the celebration. A string quartet played Vivaldi to greet the sunrise over the lake, followed by a beach clean-up at 8:00A.M.

Shunning the stagnant river and the official activities, Lily and Jay made their way down to their beloved beach for the more spontaneous celebration. Groups of elementary school children and their teachers showed up with large garbage bags and cheerfully walked the several miles of lakefront. One silly man in Bermuda shorts wandered around with a megaphone, giving orders about where to stack the recyclables. UWM students supervised a great beach-cleaning activity and the creation of "Garbage Mountain," which rose over ten feet into the sky by noon.

Jay was particularly amused by an artistic creation on the sand. "Look at this, Lily!" Somebody had made an octopus out of eight used condoms around a rusted smiley-face button.

"Far out!"

They moved aside as high school students snaked through the groups chanting, "All we are saying is give peace a chance." Small bands of roaming musicians wearing tie-dyed tee shirts with deliberately torn necklines paused along the sand with impromptu performances playing everything from bongos to clarinets.

Lenore tugged at her leash and wanted to join the musicians, but eventually resigned herself to being Little Jay's bodyguard as he sat in his stroller and took in the sights. She had her moments of glory as people came over to admire her beautiful face. She wagged mightily and tried to kiss each one individually, not always a welcome happening.

At high noon, the Poets for Peace gave a reading, although most of their poems were drowned out by portable cassette players and chattering children.

Rita, a newer member of the group who had moved from

Cleveland, was a sensational reader with her "Kaddish for Lake Erie." She had been living there a year before when the Cuyahoga River, a tributary, actually had caught fire.

"Burning Lake, napalm-baked, oil-caked maiden...." she chanted. Her voice sounded like a crystal bell and people stopped to listen.

"Great addition to the group!" Mel remarked. "At least Lake Michigan isn't dead like Lake Erie, but this should be a warning."

Blue Jay was one of the last readers, and shouted his poem through a megaphone improvised from a rolled-up magazine:

Sun
　　Sky
　　Lake
　　Sand
　　People
　　Clouds
　　Seagulls
　　Beach
　　Fish
　　Planet
　　Let's bring it down
　　All singing
　　The song
　　Of our shared earth
　　And star-swirled heavens.

Let's raise it up
　　Sun Song
　　Birds Beasts

Milwaukee
Lake Michigan
Home

NOT EVERYONE COULD HEAR; not everyone cared; but a loyal cadre of fellow poets and friends crowded around protectively and cheered after each poet read. Someone passed around a bottle of fairly decent Chianti. A couple of reefers circulated—take it or leave it, live and let live—and after the reading, the group agreed that Earth Day was a great success and should become an annual event.

Lily beamed as she spun around with Little Jay, glimpsing first the lake, then the bluff, then the lake, then her giggling son, as they twirled. Her long batik skirt swirled around her and her necklace with its small harem bells jangled pleasantly. Lily had brought a generous supply of peanut butter and jelly sandwiches and when they were dizzy from their beach dance, she dug into her backpack and brought them out. "Anybody hungry?" she called.

Several poets agreed that it was time to eat. Frank supplied a jug of apple cider, only slightly fermented; other poets pitched in with a variety of offerings such as carrot sticks and M&Ms, creating an impromptu banquet splendidly spread on a Navajo-patterned beach blanket. Since their work of the day was done and the breeze no longer felt warm—after all, it was still only April on the Lake Michigan shore—the Poets for Peace clung to the warmth of the sand and feasted beneath the diminishing springtime sun. Lily took off Little Jay's tennis shoes and Lenore and Little Jay had one last romp on the sand together.

• • •

During the walk home, Blue Jay and Lily were quiet, each comfortable in their shared solitude, and Little Jay fell asleep before his stroller reached the top of the bluff.

~

A week later, Apartment 2 still stood empty and they hadn't heard from Mr. Dreschler. They expected to find an ad in the Sunday paper, so they spent their spare time shampooing the carpets, disposing of the broken dishes and other debris, and giving the apartment a thorough cleaning. "Maybe we should contact him, Blue Jay," Lily sighed. "This isn't like him."

"No, I don't plan to invite trouble. Let's just tend to business as usual and let him call."

As they pondered their most prudent course of action as they were delving into a savory Saturday spaghetti supper, Mrs. Hopkinson called from Apartment 3. "Lily! Blue Jay! I don't like to bother you but come upstairs quickly! There's something horrible going on in Apartment 5. I think someone's being tortured or murdered right over my head."

"Mrs. Hopkinson is not an alarmist," Blue Jay proclaimed. "If she says it's an emergency, I believe her." He sighed and looked longingly at his plate filled with spaghetti and three big meatballs. "We better put this up on the stove so Lenore doesn't help herself to a banquet."

Once again, Little Josh was hoisted into the potato-sack carry under Jay's arm and they hastened to the front entrance, this time going upstairs to Apartment 3. On the way they met Larry and Lenny, just in from an evening stroll.

"What's up? What's the rush?"

"Mrs. Hopkinson called. We have to talk to her in person. There seems to be trouble in Apartment 5."

"We'll help," Larry said, without hesitation. "Mrs. Hopkinson is a great neighbor."

"C'mon, then," Lily said. "We might need some help."

Mrs. Hopkinson was at the door. "Just come in and listen first," she said. "I don't know what you'll be walking into. I don't know what to think of it. This has been going on for about half an hour already."

They huddled together in the kitchen, the back door to the fire escape cracked open.

"No! Let me alone!" a shrill voice called, choking back tears. A piercing shriek filled the landing.

"Oh, my God!" Lily whispered, looking at Blue Jay. "It sounds like Moisette! Now what's she gotten herself into?"

The voice continued. "I hate you! I hate this! How can you make me do this! It's not fair. I've been so good." Great wailing and screaming ensued. "How dare you! No! I won't pick that up. No! You can't make me," followed by sobbing and choking sounds and the methodical stamping of feet.

"What do you think, Lily? Should we call the police?"

"It's very one-sided. Maybe it's just a bad acid trip. Or peyote. Maybe the Sixers found her and fed her some of their magical brownies. I think I'll just go up and take a look at what's going on."

Lenny interjected, "I know! Since you're the caretaker, why don't you just go up the fire escape and knock on the door and say you hafta check the radiators? I'll go with you. And leave your little one down here," he smiled at the little red-headed toddler who smiled back and squirmed to get free of Lily's arms.

"Um, upstairs. Oh, sure. Check the radiators in April. What's a caretaker for?" Blue Jay paused. "Okay. But then the rest of you should stay down here and be the back-up crew. You too,

Lily. Be ready to call the police if you hear that it's getting out of hand."

"Okay."

Terrible screams and moans and sobs continued.

"Forward, march, Lenny! Let's make a lot of racket." Blue Jay and Lenny loudly clomped up the fire escape making their presence known.

The moans and sobs continued.

"I don't know what we'll find. Stand back," Blue Jay said. With a false note of friendly confidence in his voice, he announced, "Caretaker here." He abruptly pushed open the screen door.

Moisette glared at the intruders. She sat alone on a large stool in the middle of the kitchen, random dribbles and crumbs dotting her blouse. Around her, strewn on the table and on the floor, were bits of food and puddles of milk.

Eyes blazing, she looked at them in amazement.

"How dare you!" she screamed at Blue Jay and Lenny. "How dare you enter my kitchen without even knocking! You startled me!"

"Uh, sorry," Blue Jay mumbled, staring at the strange scene. "What's going on here?"

"What's going on here is none of your business. That's breaking and entering! I should have my father sue you!"

"Look, Moisette, we only meant to help you. Are you okay?"

"We thought you were being injured. Can you explain what this is all about?" Lenny gestured at the mess.

"This is a case of breaking and entering. Leave!"

"Moisette, if you had been in real trouble, you'd be thanking us," Jay countered. "Do you have any idea what this sounded like outside? Everyone was worried about you."

She began to mellow. "I have been seeing a psychiatrist who is helping me resolve issues from childhood. He's helping me chill out. He has advised me to try to re-live those early times of frustration." Her voice was hoarse from screaming.

Blue Jay and Lenny exchanged glances.

"And?"

"And so I am re-living the time when my parents made me eat with a fork and spoon. I hated it. I resented it all these years, only I just didn't remember it until now."

"So?" Blue Jay prodded her to continue. "How can I take this seriously?" he thought.

"I have a lot of repressed memories and I am just learning to deal with them. Imagine the agony parents inflict on their children with all the rules and punishments." She looked at Jay when she said that. "Who knows how you're damaging your son."

"Well, he's a little young for too many table manners yet," Jay laughed. "I think all parents give their kids plenty to get neurotic about. It's the name of the game."

My psychiatrist gave me this book to read. It's called *The Primal Scream*." She gestured to a food-spattered book folded open on the kitchen table. "This author says it's a good idea to get all the pain out and then you can move on with your life. Go back into your past and ferret out all the horrible experiences that your parents and teachers put you through. Next week I intend to work through my bad times in first grade when the teacher made me write with my right hand even though I am left-handed."

"Janov," Lenny read the author's name.

"Yes, right. And now, if you would please leave, I want to continue with this session before my roommates get home. I'm supposed to do this every day for an hour until there aren't any screams or sobs left in me and I have to report back to my psychiatrist at my next session."

Lenny and Blue Jay looked at each other, suppressing

smiles.

"We're leaving right now," Blue Jay said, "but do you think you could at least keep your door shut so the other tenants don't think someone's being tortured? One aspect of being a good neighbor is not giving them cause to believe you are being murdered. This is something parents try to teach children."

The two men quickly clattered down the metal steps of the fire escape to make their report to the others; and the now-muffled sobs and cries and screams resumed.

"Ah, sweet catharsis," Blue Jay chuckled. "Maybe we all should get together and have a scream-in."

"Not a bad idea, Jay," Mrs. Hopkinson smiled.

Jay and Lenny explained the concept of Janov's therapeutic techniques to the others. Everyone felt relieved that nothing serious was wrong, but Lily was indignant. "She has no manners."

"Good that you called, Mrs. Hopkinson; but good that we decided against calling the police. We would have all felt like fools," Jay added. "Maybe we should open up a special scream therapy chamber in the boiler room and all take turns using it."

Mrs. Hopkinson served everyone claret wine in crystal goblets and they spent a delightful hour thinking of other painful situations that could be dealt with through this new, innovative scream therapy. Larry's suggestion that actual leaders of warring countries could emote and scream at each other rather than sending troops into battle was well received, but Mrs. Hopkinson gently reminded them that just because it might work for individuals didn't mean it would work for nations.

Blue Jay then speculated, "Yes, but the pen is mightier than the sword. Maybe a battle of the poets would be better than just shapeless, shameless emoting."

"At least that would be virtually soundless and the neighbors wouldn't have to endure it," Mrs. Hopkinson smiled.

Lily felt an emptiness in her stomach from hunger, made more intense by the wine. Recalling her abandoned dinner, the image of a heaping plate of spaghetti loomed large in her mind. "After living through this, I seem to have worked up an appetite. Then after supper I might need to go to the boiler room where I won't bother anybody and try a little scream catharsis myself."

Lily and Jay returned to their plates of tepid spaghetti.

"Supper interrupted," Jay mused. "Don't worry, Lily. Just another couple more months and the semester will be over. We're almost there. Things can't get any worse," Blue Jay turned to poetry for comfort. "Like the late, over-rated T.S. Eliot never said, 'April is the cruelest month.'"

But events of the supposedly "Merry Month of May" would vehemently disprove this prediction.

CHAPTER 9

MAY

Wherein the caretakers contend with strikes, a riot, a fire, an unexpected registered letter, and a drastic change of plans.

THE DOORBELL jarred everyone awake at 7:00 AM on Friday, May 1. Lily, always a quick riser, responded abruptly to its harsh, persistent ring. “Well, I don’t think it’s anybody bringing me a May basket,” she grumbled. Throwing on her robe, she ran to the door. “Yes?”

A burly man wearing a paint-spattered outfit of coveralls and denim shirt stood at the door. “Paint contractor,” he announced. “Can you give me the keys for Apartment 2?”

“Oh? Sure,” Lily replied, heading for the keyboard. “Nice of Mr. Dreschler to let us know. What’s going on?”

A tambourine jangled from Little Jay’s small room off the kitchen.

“We have orders to paint the kitchen, living room, and

dining room, stem to stern," he replied. "Have you got it cleared out yet?"

"Sure. It's all yours. I'll be up in a few minutes."

"No need. I've got my crew and my ladders waiting in front."

Lily returned to the bedroom. "What's going on, Blue Jay? He just gave us that paint and had us paint the front bathroom. Why didn't Mr. Dreschler inform us?"

Still half asleep, he muttered, "He knew we didn't have time to paint the whole place, I guess. And we would need more time. He probably wants to get it rented this month yet, the old Scrooge. Give him a call later," he yawned.

The tambourine jangled more persistently. *Chicka-chicka-chicka, bling, bling, blang!*

"That dude's got rhythm!" Blue Jay noted as he stretched.

"Yeah, so you go change his diapers," Lily snapped.

The day had begun.

ON CAMPUS that Friday at the beginning of May there was a sense of despair. President Richard Nixon announced the expansion of the war into Cambodia, claiming the Viet Cong was using these jungles as a supply route. This declaration seemed especially harsh since the President had been hinting about a reduction of forces. Frustration and desolation hung heavily like the lake fog that enveloped the city.

Students, including vets who had served in Vietnam and had now enrolled at the university for want of a better plan, now began to assemble around campus in small, urgent knots. Students who ordinarily walked a straight course from class to class to library and home again now were filled with frustration and disbelief. Everyone had cousins or friends from high school who had been killed or wounded everyone had cousins or friends in the military in parts unknown.

Some students knew that their student draft deferments were nearing an end and dreaded the thought that they might be next in line to receive those loathsome, official-looking draft notices in their mailboxes; others took it stoically and were ready to face whatever demands their country required, although they objected to US involvement.

Everyone had seen the war on television, gazed helplessly at videos of My Lai, of villagers running through napalm. The Vietnam Vets Against the War group was holding informational meetings in the Union. There were always small groups of picketers in front of the ROTC office on the third floor of Mitchell Hall, occasionally erupting into shouting matches.

There was talk of shutting the campus down. Stink bombs and fire alarms jarred the school day. Picket lines formed and vitriol spat from all sides. When Blue Jay made his way approaching the English building, he noticed a line of angry protesters blocking the door. A feeling of urgency rose in his throat. He gulped air. He had to be in attendance since word was out that some professors were failing students who didn't show up. It wasn't simply the course grade that propelled him onward; it was having enough credits to graduate. Wanting to avoid a confrontation, he decided to go around to the utility entrance. "Undergrad experience as a work study janitorial assistant has paid off," he thought, forcing a tight little grin to console himself. Slipping inside, he made his way to the second floor. When he reached the classroom, he found a note taped to the door:

Fellow Practitioners of the Fine Art of English Prose and Poetry:

I wish to inform you that class is cancelled today, due to circumstances beyond my control. However, in support of academic zeal, literary bliss and imminent grades, I will be holding an informal literary discussion around the large table at Interabang Books on Warren Avenue this afternoon at three. I apologize for any inconvenience.

Martin Olson

BLUE JAY SHRUGGED. Was it a sign of respect for the good professor or just the fact that the notice had been overlooked that it was still posted there? He slowly slogged home.

BACK AT TANNENBAUM ARMS, Lily was worried because the building seemed to be filled with unease. She took Little Jay in the familiar potato-sack carry, under her arm and balanced on her hip, and ascended the stairs. The Sixers regularly had a steady stream of people traipsing up and down the stairs, but today there was nobody in the hall. She could hear the mimeograph machine running non-stop with strains of Dylan whining in the background. Lily stopped in to remind them that the scent of weed in the hall could lead to trouble. "The boss man is around a lot lately, supervising work on Mrs. Grant's apartment. Just be a little careful, okay?"

"Sure, Lily," Craig grinned. "We have fresh brownies. Odor-proof. Would you like one?"

"Not now. I've got too much ahead of me today."

In Apartment 5, Moisette was diligently undertaking her scream therapy, this time apparently working out the necessity of being forced to wear shoes, while Linda and Sarah were trying to study at home because there were protesters blocking the library entrance. In response to her light knock, both Linda and Sarah came to the door.

'Would you like me to talk with Moisette for you? We can order her to go down to the boiler room to scream."

"No, it's all okay, Sarah responded.

"Why do you put up with this?" Lily asked.

The two roommates just looked at each other and smiled. "Because...she's Moisette," Linda quietly said.

Lily made her way down to Apartment 2 with Little Jay still in tow, trying to appease Mr. Dreschler, who had arrived at this inopportune time to meet with the contractors about the painting job.

"No, Mrs. Davis doesn't mind the music at all. She has never once complained," she told Mr. Dreschler. "She's quite deaf, you know. And Mrs. Hopkinson works all day. And we always make sure everyone quiets down in the evening." Lily was rushing through her sentences with a higher-than-usual pitch in her voice.

"And that's a good thing. We've got to hold on to our stable tenants, Lily," Mr. Dreschler admonished. "You know, every time an apartment is vacant, it's a financial setback for the management firm. You don't seem to realize that there's a bottom line here."

Although the weather was growing warmer as the sun rose higher, Mr. Dreschler stood at attention in full business regalia, perfection broken only by the beads of sweat forming on his brow and neck. He gestured around the tarp-draped living room of Apartment 2. "This is a big financial setback, you know."

Lily shook her head wordlessly. She wanted to snap at him, "You're the one who rented it to the Grimeses, not us," but she held her tongue.

She was relieved when Blue Jay appeared, back from campus much earlier than usual. Mr. Dreschler informed them that he would be running an ad in the paper on Sunday, even if the painting wouldn't be all done. "Be sure to discourage anyone who doesn't seem to be financially secure, Jay. No more people like the Grimeses, please."

Jay nodded. "I agree. But all I did was show it and take the deposit upon your request."

"You could have discouraged them more." He frowned. "Make a judgment call. Try to do a little better for the management, okay?"

Jay saw that Mr. Dreschler would not quit until he had the last word, so he bit his tongue and nodded vehemently.

After the affairs of the morning, Lily did not attempt to go to her afternoon classes; but Blue Jay met his professor and several other students over at Interabang Books that afternoon. It seemed that several teachers were holding classes at alternate sites. The professor, a reasonable sort, realized that many students needed their credits for pending graduation requirements and military deferments. He said that they could leave any work with him in stamped envelopes with their return addresses and if classes were cancelled and the campus remained troubled, he could send the work back. In the meantime, they would meet informally at Interabang on Friday afternoons for the remaining three weeks of the semester.

The weekend passed with building chores and studies. With only four more weeks left in the school year before exams, and deadlines approaching, the only break in the monotony was a Saturday outing to Lake Park with Little Jay and Lenore. On their favorite bluff overlooking the lake, Little Jay giggled and kicked his legs as they took turns pushing him in the baby swings. Although dogs weren't allowed to run freely in the park, they had brought an extra-long rope and let Lenore romp in wide circles by the baseball diamond. For a little while they forgot about building maintenance, research paper deadlines, campus strife, and distant wars as they immersed themselves in all things blue and green and growing.

On their walk home, Blue Jay stopped abruptly in front of the kiosk by the Ben Franklin. "Look, Lily! It's Orville!"

The bold eyes of Orville Grimes, a lopsided Elvis-sneer on his lips, a strand of hair dropping down his forehead, stared out from a large poster. "LOVE ME TENDER!" Bold letters proclaimed. "Hear the songs of the great Elvis Presley emerge through the skillful renditions of his Nashville cohort, Orville Grimes." Friday, May 8, at Pinkie's Tap on Burleigh.

"*I'm all shook up.* Wanna go, Lily?"

"No, thanks," she grinned. "And let's not tell Mr. Dreschler, either. He *Ain't nuthin' but a hound dog.*"

"So, now you're stealing Lost Lenore's lines."

"Never more."

They returned home in time for a supper of chicken chili and biscuits and then more studies. Blue Jay and Lily knew that they needed to complete this chapter of their academic lives, even if classes were disrupted, so they worked diligently in spite of the grim campus atmosphere.

On Sunday, the doorbell began ringing around nine. This time, Lily and Jay were expecting the interruptions, since Mr. Dreschler had notified them. The front hall sparkled with cleanliness and smelled faintly of disinfectant, making the perfect impression for prospective tenants. By noon, a couple from West Allis had given a security deposit, pending approval from Mr. Dreschler. The husband, Rob, had rented a store on Farwell and planned to open a head shop specializing in clothes and jewelry from India. The wife, Theresa, was a high school math teacher at nearby Riverside High School, so she would be able to walk to work.

Theresa looked stately, as if from another planet, in her gossamer green gown and three strands of translucent love beads. She virtually floated from room to room, occasionally tossing her long hair over one shoulder; then another.

When they reached the small bedroom off the kitchen, Theresa declared, "This is the perfect meditation chamber! Are we allowed to paint?"

"I don't see why not," Jay answered. "You'll have to run that past Mr. Dreschler. We just keep order and tend to the building."

"I want this room saffron yellow, with a sky-blue ceiling," Theresa announced.

Rob quickly added, "Of course, I could do the painting if that's too much to ask of the landlord."

They admired the freshly shampooed carpeting and the painting in progress in other parts of the apartment. If approved, they planned to move in at the end of the month.

"Well, they're going to work out just fine, I think," Jay mused after they had gone. "I can't help worrying about the Grimeses, though. I wonder how that little kid is doing."

"Let's hang out a note saying the apartment is rented so we don't get any more interruptions," Lily said. "Time for a little peace and quiet."

"Well, at least quiet, Lily, if you take the broader view."

THE NATION ERUPTED the following Monday, May 4, during the noon hour. With National Public Radio playing in the background, Lily was making toasted cheese sandwiches; Blue Jay was chewing on a pencil in the midst of an important commentary; Lost Lenore was chewing on some Cheerios thrown off the highchair tray for her by Little Jay. The customary call-in show about healthy eating was interrupted with a special broadcast. The Ohio National Guard clashed with 2,000 Kent State students protesting the expansion of the war into Cambodia. The protesters were ordered to disperse; most refused. The Guard threw tear-gas canisters, but the crowd threw rocks at the Guard and stood their ground. "Pigs off campus!" they shouted. "We have the right to protest!" Taunts continued, and more rocks. Many other students made their way across campus, intent upon ignoring both sides, simply conducting school business as usual.

Jay and Lily exchanged glances. Jay immediately switched to a radio station playing classical music, worried that Little Jay would pick up on the trouble. He adjourned to the living room to switch on the television.

Mid-day soap operas were interrupted. At 12:22 PM, several guardsmen fired their M1 Garand rifles into an area near a parking lot. Four students were killed, nine wounded. Some of the victims were not even involved in the protest but were just trying to get to classes.

Television images of the carnage flashed and looped repeatedly. Students around the country who had grown up with a belief that America was the "land of the free and home of the brave" were horrified that this situation was playing out around them.

As the day progressed, Blue Jay and Lily moved their small television set into the dining room and watched in disbelief, while taking turns distracting Little Jay in the kitchen in an attempt to shield him from the horror. The nightmarish national crisis intensified as two black anti-war protesters were slain at Jackson State in Mississippi on the same day.

Peter and Frank stopped by with a couple of other friends. "Don't even bother to try to go to classes this week," they warned. "It's chaos up there. And what's making it even worse is so many non-students we don't even recognize are on campus adding to the turmoil."

Along with campuses across the nation, UWM antiwar groups called for a strike on May 6. A plan was in place to picket early in the morning at the main entrance of Mitchell Hall near the corner of Downer Avenue and Kenwood Boulevard. This would be followed by a march around the circumference of the campus, eventually taking over the student union as strike headquarters. From there, they would branch out into the other buildings to disrupt classes and encourage dialogue about the war.

Chancellor Martin Klotsche decreed that classes should proceed, that the campus should be a forum for open, peaceful discussion. As the crowds grew and the march proceeded, over one hundred armored police officers appeared on the scene, ready to wield their riot sticks. Ugly, sometimes violent confrontations ensued instead of the stately forum for the interchange of ideas that the chancellor had naively envisioned. In a moment of comic outrage, a young man dropped his jeans and showed his backside to the officers, while other students oinked. As the march continued and vandalism spread throughout the buildings, fire alarms were pulled and bomb threats were called in. The whole campus smelled like one big stink bomb. Demonstrators followed through with the plan that had been outlined to them earlier. With little resistance, they took over the student union.

Jay and Lily made several forays to campus for updates, although they did not hang around for long. Jay had made a practice of collecting all kinds of announcement flyers, street sheets, and other publications. He came home waving his latest acquisitions, proclaiming, "History in the making!" Finally, on May 7, the dean declared a state of emergency, purportedly so the campus officials could eject "outside agitators."

As the strike continued, most professors made arrangements to meet privately or to give grades based on midterms. Jay knew that his advanced English classes would present no problem but decided he should try to get to the German class, just in case.

When he arrived in Bolton Hall, he felt he was in a battle zone out of a science fiction book.

A few students Jay recognized from his German class were standing outside. "Are you going into class? The chancellor was on TV and cancelled classes."

Jay looked about. "They managed to bring it home," he thought, noting the smashed windows, garbage containers and desks overturned in the halls, and nonfunctioning elevators. The strikers had disrupted the central power station of the campus, so there was neither air nor light. Jay's German class met in a basement classroom, and without electricity there was only the dim light of lower-level windows filtering in.

"I think I can second guess this prof. I need my grade. I need to get through."

"Scab!" someone taunted as Jay entered the building.

True to his word, Professor Tillmanns sat at his desk like a steadfast tin soldier. Two other students, neither of whom Jay knew, were also in the room, resolutely uprighting desks and attempting to make a little island of order amid the chaos.

"*Guten Tag, Herr Haakens,*" Professor Tillmanns said in his customary fashion, as if it were just another day. He made a check in his attendance book. "We are meeting only briefly today. I appreciate the effort you three students made to be here. I have made a note of that." He sighed. "As for assignments, please continue with the Thomas Mann translation. It will be due next Thursday. If classes do not proceed—and I have heard a strong rumor as such—you can drop the translations off at my office, along with any other back assignments."

He paused. "I understand the value of peaceful protest, even though it has come down to this." He looked around at the mess and shook his head. "There is a thin line one can walk between protest and vandalism. This has gone too far. People in my homeland should have protested sooner when they saw what Hitler's henchmen were doing on Kristallnacht." He paused. "Of course, hindsight is always easier to come by than foresight. Use any extra time to search your souls." He picked up his heavy brief case and shoved back his chair. "Class dismissed. *Auf Wiedersehen.*"

Jay thought about checking in at strike headquarters in the Union, thinking it would be crowded with strikers and that he could help out in some small way. He ran into Sharkey handing out Street Sheets with updates on the situation and advice for confronting pigs and narcs, as well as what to do if arrested. Although there were some broken windows and a vandalized soda machine, things seemed calm. A few students were lounging about as if they were vacationing at a fancy hotel. Other groups were huddled in intense conversation. Someone had written "STRIKE" and drawn a clenched fist in red paint across the ballroom windows facing onto Kenwood Boulevard.

"We won this round! We're holding the union! Klotsche just closed down the campus. But now we have to plan the next step," a young man wearing a Communist star on his jacket remarked in response to Jay's puzzled expression. "This is just the beginning of the Revolution!" Jay did not recognize him but was thankful for the update.

THE "NOT-SO-MERRY-MONTH-OF-MAY" limped grimly along like a war-weary soldier slumped beneath a sack of broken dreams and body parts. Lily and Jay knew that the semester was played out, even though the last official day was May 18.

"Not with a bang, but a whimper," Jay pronounced in a fake English accent, his imitation of T.S.Eliot. He duly turned in his semester German assignments, knowing that he had jumped through all the hoops required for his graduation. His advanced writing seminar had one last meeting. Professor Wiegner invited everyone to her home on Downer Avenue for an informal reading and potluck. Although no one was required to attend, the entire group showed up, showering their professor with spring flowers and bringing all sorts of dishes to share. Jay, knowing that Lily was occupied with the interview process for her seminar, decided to make his fabulous shrimp dip, a delicacy from his bachelorhood days consisting of chopped onions, sour cream, condensed onion soup, and a can of cocktail shrimp. Along with a large bag of potato chips, this was a consummate treat.

This offering joined a table filled with a delicious array of everything from organic pizza with a thick whole-wheat crust, to cheese triangles, to pickled beets. Champagne was uncorked and everyone toasted the graduates among them.

For his final presentation, Jay had submitted a series of autobiographical poems based on the progression of the war, including the peace poem he had read for Earth Day. His final poem was a requiem in honor of the Kent State martyrs.

He began:

I see
The penitent generals walking on tin cans
March down Wisconsin Avenue at break of day
Rhythmic footfalls sounding through the morning.
They mumble
What have we done
Where have we gone
Who lurks now, mourning
In the shadows between the buildings?

Screams and wails from
Rice paddies and jungles
Explode in our ears.

ACROSS THE TOWN,
The intrepid marchers
Tromping through the campus
Make a rumpus
What have we done
Where must we go
The pigs have overtaken us
And we fall down.
Fall down.
Curse this war.

NO ONE CARRYING protest signs
Or book bags full of promises,
Carrying unborn children and unfinished assignments;
or in blood-soaked jungles far away,
Or in fear-filled, steaming swamps,
Deserves
To find an Early Armageddon
On their doorstep.
It is our duty, and our need,
To remember the brave, the quiet, the confrontational,
Those who shouted
Those who quietly faced their fears,
Those who marched, who carried signs, who spat out "Pig!"
Who prayed "End the War"
Who vowed "Hell, no!"
or

Who simply tried to go to class on a sunny day,
Who bled on the pavement by a fountain,
Who saved a candy bar to share with a friend after lunch,
Who planned on going for a basketball pick-up game in the gym,
Who needed to memorize the future tense of "to be" in French,
Who was feeling the kick, kick of baby feet in the womb,
Whose shoes pinched with a blister at the heel,
Whose girlfriend was waiting in the union,
Whose mother was waiting in her beat-up Ford to give a ride
To a part-time job at the Stop 'n' Shop....

MAY ALL REST IN PEACE.
The cruel severance
The unfair price
The unjust deaths
And
May we carry on with kindness to the poor souls
Who cry out names in their sleep
Who put on their sweaters and pick up the signs
And sigh and cry and call out
End the war!

WE ARE all children
Borne of war
Who say
No more!
This is our age
As we rage

As we engage without surcease
To
Wage
Peace

THERE WAS a moment of silence when he finished, followed by spontaneous applause. Jay looked around at the familiar faces of the group—many who had begun as strangers but had become friends over the course of the year. "It's over," he thought. "It's the end. I did it. No, we did it."

He smiled. "Thank you."

At that point, a large, black-and-white spotted rabbit hopped into the room and everyone burst out laughing.

"Never mind. That's my mentor, Virginia, named after Virginia Woolf. You know. A wolf in rabbit's clothing," Professor Wiegner said. "She's tame. She lives here, too. Has a room of her own."

Several other students read excerpts from longer prose works, as well as poems. Frank read a long excerpt from his novel, still not finished but already over 75,000 words, he proudly announced. Although Rosie had not taken the class, she came along as a guest of Frank. Someone had brought the new Paul McCartney album, and it provided background to conversation. Jay secretly had little use for The Beatles, even though Paul apparently had little use for them, either, having announced the dissolution of the group in April; but Jay kept his opinion to himself. Wine and conversation flowed, covering topics from Nixon to nihilism to the bathroom habits of rabbits and everything in between. The evening ended with hugs all around and promises to stay in touch.

. . .

Lily had given much effort to her final collaborative project for her sociology seminar and was feeling short-changed that she and Pam would not be able to share their results with the group. The teacher had no heart for continuing past the officially decreed end of the semester and told her students to submit written summaries of their research. "What about learning for learning's sake? It really isn't all about the grade, is it?"

Pam shrugged. "Maybe it's all about being done with this place." She looked around at the boarded-up windows in the Union and shrugged. "I can't say that I blame her."

For her part, Lily had interviewed Klara Werner and Mrs. Davis about their formative experiences. Lily wondered why she hadn't asked these questions in the general course of relationships and was fascinated by their stories.

Mrs. Davis spoke about her upbringing at the turn of the century. The results were surprising, not the least that Mrs. Davis was willing to talk so freely. She was an only child, as she put it, "the apple of her father's eye;" born in Wyoming in 1890, the year Wyoming joined the United States. Her father ran a general store, but her mother was from a nearby farm family.

"We girls were expected to be pious and submissive. Girls were generally given just a basic education up to third grade, because our lot in life was to someday be a good wife and mother. I took to schooling real well, so I stayed at it through the eighth grade. There were only three girls in my eighth grade graduation class of twenty-two."

Lily was an avid listener, and once Mrs. Davis started talking, she continued without any more encouragement than a nod. Lily and Pam had prepared their list of questions, but Lily intuitively put it aside; Mrs. Davis was covering the topic better than Lily could have planned.

"I married my childhood sweetheart in 1913. I was already getting up in years, twenty-three, for a marriageable Wyoming lady. I took to the land. I knew how to plow a straight furrow and milk a cow, and we were planning to take over my grandparents' farmstead one day. Sometimes I miss that place." Her voice trailed off.

"Louie and I had a grand church wedding; I was fitted with an ivory silken gown and my hair was marcelled and worn high in a pompadour. I could show you our wedding picture sometime."

Lily was curious about Mrs. Davis's first voting experience. "Did you first vote in 1920 when women got the vote?"

"Lord, no! In Wyoming women already had the vote! We kept it when we joined the union. I guess the founders recognized that homestead women shared the work fifty-fifty, and it was never a question for us to vote or not to vote."

All this information was new, and Lily scribbled notes on her yellow legal pad. With the outbreak of WWI, Mrs. Davis's husband felt it was his obligation to enlist, to make the world safe for democracy. She said goodbye to him at the train station in Cheyenne, and never saw him alive again. His body came home in a wooden box and he was buried in a flag-draped coffin in St. Mark's cemetery, next to the church where they had been married. "That was the saddest day of my life."

After a decent period of grieving, she decided that she wanted to start her life over in a new place. The farmstead was no longer an option, and the thought of spending the rest of her life helping out in the family's general store did not appeal. Her mother's older sister's daughter lived in Milwaukee and wrote to her about a secretarial position at an insurance company. She invited her cousin to stay with her until she could get up on her feet; so one day in Spring of 1919, she boarded the Cheyenne train for Chicago, then took the streetcar to Milwaukee.

Here she joined her cousin's Christian Science Church and found a community of supportive friends. "Role of women? Just be strong and eat healthy foods and live by your conscience and follow your instincts. Oh, say your prayers and never give up on your walking. Look at me. Eighty-eight years old and still going strong. God helps those who help themselves." She nodded, pleased at her own wise comments.

"Look at you, in your t-shirt and blue jeans. Women today have it easier, a more relaxed life style. At your age, I had to have help in the morning getting into a boned corset. We'd pull them tight, and our bosoms would rise and our behinders would stick out. We were like caged pigeons."

Lily immediately thought of the connections between women's fashion and the degrees of freedom one's clothing afforded—all tied up with societal views of womanhood. This was her kind of sociology, not the charts and statistics. She planned to do more research about this.

"I wish my father's camera had arrived. I could have taken a good picture of Mrs. Davis to supplement the interview." The thought stirred excitement as Lily envisioned an entire book of interviews with a diversity of women, illustrated by close-range, black-and-white photographs.

She smiled at Mrs. Davis, who looked to Lily like a timeless noblewoman, sitting with erect posture in her worn gray sweater and gathered skirt. She thought to herself, "This woman is in her own way perfect."

Mrs. Davis picked up her cane, signaling the end of the meeting. "I need to get over to the grocery store before they close. You come back any time, Lily. Any time."

"I'm getting a camera that was my dad's," Lily spoke her thoughts. "Could I take your picture sometime?"

"Because I'm so gorgeous? I guess I would let you if you don't think I'll break the camera."

They proceeded down the stairs together, Mrs. Davis with her cane in one hand and a wicker shopping basket in the other.

Two days later the interview with Klara started slowly. Her English was good, but she retained a heavy accent. "Too bad Jay didn't know you spoke German when he started a German class first semester. He really struggled at the beginning," Lily remarked.

At first Klara was reluctant to speak of her past, but as Lily gently persisted, she began to speak of her early life. Born in 1910, Klara had lived through the First World War, as well as the dreadful days of near starvation and inflation under the Weimar Republic. "Did you know we had to pay a million marks for a loaf of bread?" During the Depression, things got even worse. When she was 23, she had an offer to come to the United States as a translator of legal documents. Over her family's objections, she was only too glad to leave the Homeland behind. On the morning of her train departure to get to the harbor at Bremerhaven, her mother gave her a gold ring with a garnet stone that had been her grandmother's. Klara held out her right hand and showed Lily the ring. "As you can see, I have taken good care of it."

Lily asked her about child rearing. "All children learned manners and to respect elders. Children were to be seen and not heard. Girls were told that they should be concerned about three things: '*Kinder, Küche, und Kirche.*' That's *kids, cooking, and church*. I was lucky that my parents appreciated a good education, and I went to the *gymnasium*—which is what we call high school—rather than put out to learn a trade. That was a modern view, but we still wore long skirts and never showed our knees. That would have been for the wild girls in Berlin. Movie stars and prostitutes."

Klara met Ernie at a friend's birthday party when she was 26. She and Ernie had one son. "We raised him to be a good man. But we had a sharp division of the jobs. Ernie never changed a diaper and I never pounded a nail in the wall to hang a picture. He never washed a dish or a stick of clothing in his life. I learned how to tend the boiler, because what would we do if we needed a back-up? But I never shoveled a single flake of snow, all these years. Peter helped his father with chores when he was older. If Peter needed a reprimand, it was Ernie's job, too. Sometimes he'd take a paddle to Peter, but only lightly on his backside to teach a lesson. Peter was really a good boy, and now he is an attorney with a Milwaukee law firm working with the son of one of the lawyers I worked for. They were in law school together at Marquette."

Although she was fond of Klara, Lily found much to disagree with in Klara's approach to child rearing, personally being an advocate of time-outs and gentle redirection rather than corporal punishment of any sort. She had to remind herself that she was conducting an interview and her role was to gather information, not to engage in conversation. Realizing that Mrs. Davis and Klara had been born half a world apart, twenty years apart, and raised in two markedly separate cultures, she was fascinated with the differing views they represented.

Although it was not planned, Pam's and Lily's interviews were perfect complements. Pam had interviewed her mother, Alice, now in her early fifties, about growing up during the Depression. Alice was frugal, not afraid to speak her mind on any subject, and very independent-minded. Her family had never taken welfare, no matter how hard up they were. Pam's grandmother had opened a little shop in their living room since they were located on a busy street in West Allis. Alice and her brother had helped in any way they could, even standing outside the storefront selling a newspaper called *The Grit* for five cents apiece. Alice enjoyed that, especially sneaking off to read the serialized adventure stories that were on the back page.

Through it all, Alice vowed that she would never be poor again. She worked her way from salesclerk in the bargain basement of Sears Roebuck to an assistant managerial position in women's wear. "I had to work twice as hard as a man to be promoted to management, and I never took a day off no matter how sick I felt or how much I wanted to stay home."

One day a tall, somber man came in and asked for help selecting a dress for his mother. Alice recalled, "I helped him pick out a paisley print dress, cotton, with a delicate lace collar. I remember that dress in every detail. Turns out, his mother loved that dress. And I fell hard for Jude, and I guess it was mutual." It was the beginning of a great relationship that produced four children, Pam being the youngest. "I remember her wearing that dress, Pam. Your grandmother."

Three years ago, just when the children were all out of the nest, Alice and Jude were planning a trip to New York City. One Thursday night he did not come home from work as expected. Alice received a phone call. Her husband was in critical condition in the hospital, having had a heart attack on the job. The next day he passed.

The children rallied around their mother, but the situation called for all her inner strength to face life alone without him. "Morning after morning after morning," she said. "I miss him every day, Pam." She paused. "In spite of my complaining about our childcare arrangement, I think of my little grandchild Maggie as a blessing in my life. She has her grandpa's big, silly grin, and I am making sure she will always know about him. I've read about feminism nowadays. I am not a feminist;

Imagine me without a bra! I'm independent of any movement. I'm a womanist who loves her own and her home."

Pam laughed. "Maybe you're both, Mom, bra or no bra." She resisted an impulse to lecture her mother about holding an over-simplified outlook on feminism.

Pam smiled, recounting this rare confession to Lily. "Now I look at my mother with new appreciation. Especially that Depression part. I even understand better why she keeps a pantry full of canned soup and saves balls of string and old clothes that 'might come in handy someday.'"

Pam also had a friend, Jo, active in SHREW, and interviewed her for the research project.

Lily looked puzzled, so Pam explained. "I know, it's hard to keep up on all the groups popping up. You gotta read your *Kaleidoscope* a little closer, Lily That's an acronym for Students Hell-bent on Relevant Education Reform, or something like that. The group was meeting with the Dean of the School of Education to propose a daycare facility on campus for fall. My friend Jo said she viewed childcare as both a personal and political issue, since women bore most of the responsibility for childcare, and this would help equalize the situation for students with children. Also, the daycare center would feature something she considered of utmost importance: women communicating and bonding with other women for everyone's good.

"Too often women have been pitted against each other, trying to look the prettiest or snag the handsomest dude. Even academically, some people don't consider it cool for a woman to appear too smart. And then there is the way some professors treat women,"

Pam questioned Jo at length about the formation of her views. Jo had grown up in a wealthy suburban family, but when she became pregnant at sixteen, her parents wanted to send her away to live with an aunt in California and give up the baby and return like nothing had happened except enjoying an 'exchange student semester.' She had run away and lived on the streets for a couple weeks until she couldn't take it any longer. Fortunately, there was another aunt, this one on Milwaukee's Lower East Side, who took her in. Now she and her son were living with this sympathetic aunt who said she and her son could live there with free room and board, as long as she was stayed in school and didn't use drugs.

As Lily read over Pam's work, she remarked, "This is too much to just bury away. I think we need to get the class together anyway and have a long discussion. It's all out here. Great, ground-breaking work. Far out. Very far out."

"Do you think we should try to convene the class, anyway?" Pam asked.

"No one else is doing anything like this. Maybe we should co-teach a class through the Free University. We could call it "Modalities of Mothering."

Pam wryly answered, "Or "The Perseverance of Women in the Twentieth Century."

"I would be happy to be part of that. Maybe we could encourage everybody to bring their children along. It might be a little crazy, but we could all see mothering in action."

"Does Dr. Spock Rock?"

"Hey, Mom, Let Baby Outta the Refrigerator!"

"Too Cool!"

"Hey, Papa, I Ain't no Fridgerater Mama!"

"Realistically, Pam, I have to wait and see where I am in the fall. Let's keep it in the realm of possibility."

Blue Jay's complimentary three copies of *Undercurrents*, as well as letters of acceptance from both the University of Chicago and the University of Iowa, arrived on the same day, a bright mid-month Wednesday. While the University of Chicago did not offer any financial assistance, Paul Engel's Writers' Workshop in Iowa offered him a teaching assistantship. Because of the clouds around graduation and his general disenchantment with the university scene, Blue Jay was having second thoughts about his academic future. "Maybe I should just take a year off and get a job," he mused. "Or still try for a teaching assistantship at UWM for fall. I wouldn't mind working with Dr. Webster. The man's a classic; predictable and scholarly, and he made the offer. Anyway, how important is it for a writer to have a master's degree? Maybe we should just stay in Milwaukee and I'll get a job in a bookstore and bring home a paycheck and never sell blood again and just write and read. Writers write."

"Maybe stay..." Lily agreed. "Then I could go back to UWM in the fall for one last time and get my teaching certificate in Social Studies. Not really my first choice, but I'd only need one more semester and then student teaching. Let's think about it."

The following day, early afternoon as Little Joshua was napping, the well-padded package from Lily's mother arrived. The camera! Lily stared at it, trying to form a memory. Her father's camera. His hands had touched it. He had used it as a tool to capture images from his world. He was the last person to use it. She closed her eyes, holding it close.

"This is no Brownie Flash Camera," she thought. "I really don't know the first thing about real cameras, but I can learn. I *will* learn. Maybe somebody from the Free University can teach me, or maybe some photographer on the *Kaleidoscope* staff."

She spotted the manila envelope of pictures still in the box. One by one, she spread them out on Mrs. Grant's hand-me-down kitchen table. They were black and white images with a matte finish. Some had crinkled edges. Pictures of her as a baby, as a toddler in a laundry basket with underpants on her head like a bonnet; by a flower bed in a frilly dress holding her mother's hand; sitting in a wagon with arms outstretched towards the photographer, smiling....

Not all the pictures were of this nature. There were about thirty photos of what looked to be plundered fields and destroyed houses; of helmeted soldiers lounging on a hillside, rifles nearby; of landscaped meadows with grazing pigs; of airplanes and jeeps. She noticed the eyes, always the eyes, trusting, alert, sometimes defiant, but staring right into the lens. Lily noted that her father must have made that kind of deeply personal contact with his subjects before taking the pictures.

Although Lily looked for a photo of her father, there was none. "In actuality, he is there, though, in every picture, on the other side that you can't see. This is the world through his eyes. And now he is here."

She sat staring at the pictures, absorbing them, her mind too overflowing with these images to make sense out of them. Somehow at this moment she knew that she would become a sociologist armed with a camera, an interviewer, a cultural observer, documenting the present. Damn Professor Milton and all his ilk. She would continue to write well—for a human; she would pursue her advanced degree in sociology.

When Jay came home, she was still sitting there, holding her camera, rearranging the pictures. "This is a new day for me, Jay," she said, rushing into his arms. "This was my past and now it will be my future."

As the month progressed, many professors and students seemed to vanish into Lake Michigan fog with no formal closure. Grades were awarded on the basis of assignments completed as of May 4, or even at midterm. Other staunch traditionalists such as Blue Jay's German professor insisted upon a final exam in spite of the chancellor's recommendation.

Blue Jay crossed the threshold of Bolton Hall without any smoke bombs being set off and only one brief fire alarm blaring. The examination period was held in a nearly abandoned classroom, quiet except for the sound of workers outside repairing damaged windows. Power had been restored and lights and elevators were working again. Many of his fellow students had chosen to take failing grades rather than show up for the exam, but others were there because they knew they could be drafted if their grade point sank too low. Days earlier someone had written *SCAB* on the chalkboard in big letters, and nobody even bothered to erase it. Blue Jay sat hunched over the small desk and wrote in his most legible script, turning in the test as quickly as he could with only a polite nod in the direction of the professor.

Sporadic protests continued, but overall the campus settled back to angry grumbles of frustration, mistrust and recrimination.

Jay 's final Contemporary Lit class met at Interabang Bookshop for one last time. "This is the way the world ends, not with a bang but a whimper," his professor ruefully quoted T.S.Eliot. "You students have put in a lot of work this semester, in spite of all the goings-on here. Let us hope that your insights into present-day authors will deepen your character. Somehow, in all the protests and looking outward, we Americans seem to have forgotten to look inward upon our souls." He paused. "My hope for each one of you is that you will continue to read critically and think deeply. Now more than ever, we need these qualities in our youth."

The rest of the class consisted of sharing final research papers and offering gentle critiques. Jay had crashed his paper at the last minute, staying up all night to finish, and presented a sound analysis of Allen Ginsberg's "Howl." No one felt like arguing.

Lily wasted no time figuring out the basics of her camera. Her mother had thoughtfully included three rolls of film, each with a 36-picture capacity. She decided to use the film sparingly, since it was expensive and developing was even worse; but the camera bug had bitten her and she was never without it around her neck.

After another blood-selling excursion to the West Side, Jay stopped in at Renaissance Book Shop on Wisconsin Avenue. The gracious proprietor, George John, held court in a magnificent, high-backed antique chair. Jay inhaled the inky, slightly musty, old-leather book smell, gazed at the narrow rows of shelves stacked high with books of all shapes and sizes; and could have browsed and conversed for hours, but he was a man with a mission: "Do you happen to have any old camera books or manuals?"

The proprietor led Jay to a dusty box containing all types of old manuals for everything from mimeograph machines to Model-T repair. "It's your guess what's in there."

Jay hit the jackpot, discovering a manual for the Leica M3, a 35mm rangefinder camera. "This looks like her camera. I think this might be it!" The pamphlet had a diagram naming all the parts in English and German. It explained how to adjust the manual focus and exposure and made suggestions for varying distances. "Lily will love this! How much?"

The proprietor looked up from his poetry book. "That's one dollar, if you don't mind. You've bought a lot of books from me over the past few years. You deserve a deal. By the way, if you find any great old books at a rummage or estate sale, just bring them in and maybe you can trade them for store credit. But no Reader's Digest Condensed Books, please."

That evening, Jay presented the manual ceremoniously, and Lily devoured joyfully, page by page. Although the manual was for a somewhat newer model, most of the information was the same. Lily felt empowered.

"Before we go up north, I will take representative pictures of everything—Lake Michigan, friends, my Big and Little Joshuas, Messy Bessie, and Mitchell Hall. Oh, and I need a clear shot of Tannenbaum Arms from across the street to catch all three floors; and even the back fire escape landing going down to our English Basement."

"And what about the great Kewaunee boiler?" Jay prodded.

"And the boiler. Of course. Right on! I am going to use this Leica to document our lives."

On the day Blue Jay received his hard-won diploma through the mail, Lily, Little Jay and Blue Jay celebrated with a trip to his favorite restaurant, Ma Fischer's, for hamburgers and chocolate malted milk shakes.

Jay's former roommate from back in his Brady Street days turned up with his present girlfriend. Lily and Jay recalled how he always had a series of women involved in intense relationships that never seemed to last more than a month. Astonishingly, Ronald had changed his image completely. His previous hippie attire was gone, replaced by a slickly groomed hairdo. Both he and his girlfriend were wearing twin unisex outfits of black, lace-trimmed bell bottoms and orange shirts hanging open at the neck. When they moved on, promising to get together soon, Lily remarked, "I think this must be the real thing for Ronald. Why else would he go all out with that costume?" Both laughed.

"He used to be the hippest hippie, Lily. Now this."

"Not to change the subject, Jay, but you must feel great! You never have to speak another word of German again if you don't want to, and you can decide what you want to do next. Congratulations again!"

"Do you think the campus life will change? Would all the

student protest in the world make a difference?" Jay mused. "This has been a rough year all around. But you know, I think we made a dent."

"We have borne witness in our own fashion," Lily pontificated. "Not everybody has to carry a protest sign. Someone has to make the peanut butter and jelly sandwiches and mop up. That would be me. Someone has to be a scribe and honor the documents and speak for the era. That would be you. And now I have my camera, better than a hundred protest signs for me."

"We've been underground people in more ways than one, Lily. It's not over yet. The struggle continues. We continue."

She wiped the grease off her fingers and went for her camera. "Smile, Joshua. This is history." Almost one year old now, Little Jay was figuring out that when his mother pointed her camera in his direction, he was supposed to smile. He beamed at her and kicked his feet in the booster chair.

"I don't really know what I'm doing with this camera yet, but now that I have the manual I feel a little more confident," Lily said. "I hope some of these turn out."

Jay smiled. "I have never known you to fail at anything you really put your mind to."

"FINALLY, I think we're in for a peaceful weekend, at least at Tannenbaum Arms," Blue Jay remarked, as they left the restaurant and pushed Little Jay's stroller through the streets. "I think the UWM protesters are all either played out or getting ready for the next round somewhere. Or off to San Francisco for the summer. Let's go down to the lake before we go home."

As they passed Water Tower Park, they paused to sit by the fountain. Only a few other people were there, mostly couples in deep conversation. One man had removed all his clothes, and was basking naked in the fountain, but everyone ignored him like it was the most natural sight in town; and it was. Jay was tempted to snatch the clothes and hide them as a joke but thought better of it.

"Look up, Lily!" Blue Jay announced. "Little Jay, see the wizard up there?" He pointed up towards the top of the tall, whitewashed water tower. "I see his pointy cap with the moon and stars on it, and he has a big pair of binoculars!"

"Sure, Jay. Sure. I see him, too!" Lily played along.

"He's the Great Wizard of the East Side. He is looking over the whole neighborhood, keeping watch on all of us, to keep us safe!"

"He's wearing a purple cape with sparkles all over it! He's leaning out right now! Do you see him, Jay and Jay?"

Little Jay looked up and lifted up his hands; then since they had momentarily set him free from his stroller, he took off for the fountain.

Jay snatched him up and stuck him back in his stroller. "Let's get moving here so we can watch the moon rise over the lake."

Infatuation with Lake Michigan ran deep within them, although Jay staunchly held his preference for Lake Superior. Even Lake Michigan was tranquil as the moon rose, creating an intangible silver path from horizon to shore. "Hey, Blue Jay, let's walk across to Michigan."

"You bet. Better yet, let's just wait and next month drive up to the Upper Peninsula."

"Yeah, I know. Yooper Paradise. Lake Superior. Now, there's a real lake."

"This is lake enough for me. Right on!"

This comfortable interchange continued as they strolled back to Tannenbaum Arms in the dusk.

. . .

As they turned off Oakland Avenue, however, they noticed flashing red lights and billowing smoke. Tannenbaum Arms was burning!

"O my God!" Lily cried, as they hastened their steps.

"I hope somebody got Mrs. Davis out," was Blue Jay's first thought.

"And Lost Lenore and Messy Bessie!"

As they approached the building, they noticed that the street was cordoned off. There were two fire trucks and an ambulance. They saw Larry and Lenny with Mrs. Davis. A fireman was trying to persuade Mrs. Davis to get into the ambulance and get checked out, but she was adamantly refusing. Mrs. Hopkinson, Moisette, and a cluster of other people were on the sidewalk across the street, helplessly, silently watching. Klara and Ernie had come and were standing somberly on the sidelines. "Every super's worst nightmare," he shook his head.

"Everybody's out," Larry said. "It seems to be confined to Apartment 6."

"The Sixers! And where are they?" Jay looked around.

"They took off to God only knows where," said Linda. "I'd hate to be in their shoes right now."

"O my God!" Lily cried again. "Our dog and our bird! I'm going in for Lenore and Messy Bessie. Watch Little Jay. And Lenny, watch my camera!" She tore off and slyly crossed the street in an attempt to slip past the barricade to get to the rear of the building unnoticed.

"Wait! Watch the baby, Larry. I'm going, too!" Blue Jay said; but Lily was already making her way past the striped roadblock that had been placed in the center of the street. Little Jay started howling in his stroller. Klara saw what was happening and came over and lifted him out. "*Alles ist Gut, Kindchen,*" she crooned.

A police officer grabbed Lily by the wrist as Blue Jay reached her. "Not so fast, Sister."

"Our dog's in there! And our bird!" she shrilled.

"Madam, you'll have to let the firemen handle it," he said. "Anyway, they're probably okay down there. Fire burns up, not down, and we've got this here under control."

"I've got to go! They're precious!"

The police officer hesitated, "In fact, give me your key and wait here. I'll go check."

Lily acquiesced and looked at Blue Jay, "This could have been a whole lot worse. But you know, we'll catch the brunt of this." She swooped up their howling toddler and gave him a big hug.

Moments later, Lost Lenore came bounding up, yelping and trying to jump up and kiss everyone on the lips at once; the officer emerged carrying a barking Messy Bessie in her cage.

"Everything's fine down there. Not even any smell of smoke. But if this makes you feel better, here are your buddies."

The officer noticed the parakeet for the first time. "A barking bird? Now I've heard it all."

Blue Jay peered up at the third floor, "Oh, venerable Samuel Tannenbaum, what do you think of your building now? Are you rolling over in your grave?"

"On a more practical note," Lily asserted, "What will Mr. Dreschler think?"

"Whose turn is it to call him?" Blue Jay asked.

All the tenants were allowed back into the building except for the Apartment Sixers, who managed to reappear as the fire trucks pulled away. Their apartment had suffered only minor fire damage in the living room area, but extensive smoke damage throughout the front half of the apartment. Lily and

Blue Jay generously offered to let Mel, Dan, and several other of their unidentified consorts sleep in their living room, but Mel said they would rather go over to Bongo Bob's new pad where they could smoke a few joints to calm their rattled nerves.

Before they left again, Blue Jay dealt sternly with them. "I need to know exactly what went on—how this started. Who was in the apartment. Full names and addresses. Where you can be reached. We owe that much to Mr. Dreschler." Lily had never seen Jay this furious.

"Um, it's a long story," began Mel. "We were all in the other room, working out the next news release at the typewriter beside the mimeograph machine."

"And?"

"We're not really sure, but somebody must have left some candles burning in the living room and they caught the curtains on fire," clarified Dan.

"But nobody knows who. Or if. For sure."

"Because there might have been a joint left in the ash tray, not really put out. But since it was in the ash tray, how could that have caused a fire?"

They were all talking at once, and Jay was having trouble keeping all the explanations straight.

"And we were all in the far back of the pad, so we didn't even smell it til it was pretty bad and the curtains were starting to go up."

"And then we called the fire department and took off."

Jay had been worried and alarmed at first, but at this explanation, he became angry. "You could have burned the whole place down to the ground!"

"Next time we'll be more careful," Mel tried to apologize, and sounded truly devastated.

"There will be no next time for you," Jay declared.

. . .

LILY HAD the honor of calling Mr. Dreschler, who came over the next morning to survey the damage, shaking his head. He chose to shun Lily and Blue Jay, except for reminding Lily that she still owed him for the dry-cleaning bill from the time the handle broke off the mug and spilled all over his suit and woolen overcoat.

His ultimate response arrived the following Monday morning in the form of a registered letter:

MR. AND MRS. JOSHUA HAAKENS: You are hereby given notice of termination as caretakers of Tannenbaum Arms due to negligence in fulfillment of your duties. Please be informed that you must vacate the apartment within 30 days. Please be sure to leave the vacuum cleaner, all unused cleaning supplies, and a check for $23.50 to cover the dry-cleaning expenses to my clothing caused by your carelessness.

Sincerely,

Mr. Oscar Dreschler

SPEECHLESS AT FIRST, Blue Jay and Lily stared at each other. Then they mutually burst out in laughter. "End of June! That's when we wanted to go up to the UP anyway!" Blue Jay snorted.

"Why are we laughing?" Lily snickered.

"Insanity. Euphoria, Lily!"

"What about our stuff?"

"It'll work out. There's always Franko's parents' garage."

"Oh. Yeah."

Jay laughed. "Let's not wait that long. I'll call my parents. Tell 'em to get the upstairs ready. Or maybe the cabin. I don't need any ceremony or party. I have the diploma."

"Don't stick me in a cabin unless there's a flush toilet."

"Oops! Not the cabin, then."

"How many days until June? Let's get packing."

"Three. No. Blue Jay. You're moving too fast for me. Maybe we could still leave later--mid-June or end of June. We have to go to the Ben Franklin dumpster and start getting some boxes. And we need some time to line things up for July. We're not staying up there, you know." The voice of practicality triumphed over impulse; and perhaps the benevolent ghost of old Samuel Tannenbaum had a few surprises in store for them before their departure.

Jay's parents sent a postcard that they both signed, expressing joy that their wayward son was coming home. There was always work at the restaurant or working in the truck garden.

"What do they think? That Little Jay and I are some of your little trophies of conquest?" Lily asked.

"Well, if they think that, they'll change their minds as soon as they meet you."

A couple days later a postcard arrived addressed to Lily. "We are looking forward to your visit. We welcome you as our own daughter. Come whenever you want and stay as long as you want. Love, Mom and Dad Haakens"

Lily felt better after reading that message. Maybe, just maybe, she would enjoy life in Mosquitoland, she opined. But already her thoughts were moving ahead to the challenges of September.

CHAPTER 10

JUNE

Wherein the caretakers of Tannenbaum Arms take their farewell.

A RENTED U-haul trailer had been attached to Pete's old Buick and several members of the Poets for Peace helped relocate the round oak table, the carved chairs, the wicker couch, the television set, and other treasured items in Frank's family garage until such time as Blue Jay, Lily, and Little Jay could return to Milwaukee and find a new home. Ernie Werner who had done so much to teach them about boiler operation and building maintenance was sympathetic when he heard about their eviction notice and said he would offer them a good recommendation. He knew another building super who was moving to Arizona for his arthritis and would see if it would work out for them if they decided they wanted to stay in Milwaukee and take on another building.

Lily had found the perfect well-paying summer job beginning in early August, working with her friend Pam in a county parks program. They would be leading puppet-making groups and creating puppet shows which the children would put on in Lake Park and the East Side Library. Pam's daughter Molly and Little Jay would be able to come along, too. Blue Jay had talked to George John, owner and chief proprietor of the venerable Renaissance Book Store on Wisconsin Avenue, who agreed to hire him on a temporary basis, with promise of full employment in the fall if things worked out. Although he had notified the University of Chicago that he would not be attending, he still kept the door open for Iowa. He and Lily needed to make this decision by June 30, and Blue Jay thought that being in the UP might help him get more perspective on their situation. The UWM option kept looking more inviting and he submitted an application for a teaching assistanceship. "After all, I feel really like I belong here." He paused. "Milwaukee is home."

Lily nodded her agreement. "Home."

Another postcard of a rugged stone shoreline beside a waterfall arrived addressed to Lily. It was from Blue Jay's sister: "We are waiting for you. Tell my brother I miss him. No good fights with anybody lately. Guess who. XOXOX".

Jay looked at the card. "You're getting deluged with cards. No pun intended. That's Bond Falls. There's an ice cream shop there with the best ice cream in the Upper Peninsula. We'll go there."

Messy Bessie had a new temporary home with Linda in Apartment 5, with the promise that she would be reunited with them at the end of July. Lost Lenore would come with them to Marquette, Michigan; this issue hadn't even been moot.

On the day before their departure, a mid-June morning, Lily and Blue Jay had said their good-byes, making the rounds of the apartments. Mrs. Davis had solemnly shaken hands and wished them well, then had given them a quart of her home-made garlic-seasoned dill pickles, along with s small book of the teachings of Mary Baker Eddy. "This is the key to the secret of good health and long life," she proclaimed. She picked up her cane and walked them out into the hall, seeming as reluctant to see them leave as they were to part with her.

"We will be back to visit you a lot, Mrs. Davis," Lily promised. "I still want to take a good picture of you." She added to herself, "But I will never forget you."

Larry and Lenny gave them a copy of *Gertie the Duck*, inscribed with the message: "Presented to the best caretakers ever to grace the Tannenbaum Arms with their presence. We hope you and Little Joshua will enjoy this story through the years."

The new tenants in Apartment 2 were just settling in, painting their meditation chamber and setting up their stereo system. "This place sure doesn't look the same," Lily remarked. "It's amazing, how each unit is different, taking on the personality of the dwellers."

In her thoughts, she went back to Mrs. Grant, then moved on to the Grimeses. So much had happened here in less than a year.

Moisette was off on her European juggernaut, but Linda and Lisa took Messy Bessie's cage in hand and placed it in the center of the dining room table. "We never eat in here, anyway," Linda said. "We'll take good care of this feathered squawker-bird, and you take good care of my little Jaybird." She reached for his hand and shook it.

"His red hair in the sunlight looks like a bright halo," Linda laughed. "I suppose you'll have to cut it one of these days, though."

Mr. Dreschler did not receive a check for his dry cleaning, but they left him a terse note explaining that they would not be returning, that the boiler had been cleaned and shut down for the summer and the vacuum cleaner was awaiting the next caretakers in the cleaning supply storage bin next to the boiler room. "I never did turn that old coal bin into my meditation chamber," Lily attempted to joke.

As they placed the note on the boiler room door, Lily said, "I don't suppose I'll ever get my marked quarters out of that washer, though." She envisioned a last wild act of insurrection, prying open the box beneath the coin slot and grabbing a fistful of coins. "Maybe Mr. Dreschler can put those quarters towards his dry-cleaning bill."

EARLY THE NEXT MORNING, on the designated day of departure, Lily and Blue Jay paused in the middle of the sidewalk in front of the red brick building. If you glanced at them, you would never think they were anything other than random passers-by. If you looked a bit closer, what seemed to be a navy-blue book bag was in actuality a canvas and aluminum back carrier with a toddler perched in it sitting upright like a little prince. As for the nondescript mutt tugging on the leash beside them, it might get a second look just because it seemed to be such an odd combination of spaniel, beagle, setter, and perhaps even dachshund....

"WAIT!" Lily said as Blue Jay strapped Little Jay into the newly purchased baby seat for their rental car. "I forgot something!"

She disappeared around the side of the building. A couple minutes later she returned, proudly carrying two framed documents. "It's our boiler operator's licenses. You never know."

Blue Jay smiled at her. “I know. 97%. Superior boiler operator. We were extraordinary caretakers. Extraordinary.”

“Ha!”

Blue Jay whistled to Lost Lenore, who needed no second invitation to jump in the back seat next to Little Jay. They climbed in. The car pulled away.

ABOUT THE AUTHOR

Author and historian Darlene Wesenberg Rzezotarski has based this novel on personal experiences, supplemented by articles from a variety of small press newspapers including *Kaleidoscope* and *Street Sheet*. With a master's degree in comparative literature and many years of teaching experience to draw upon, she has created endearing characters inhabiting the transformational era of the Vietnam War.

www.ingramcontent.com/pod-product-compliance
Lightning Source LLC
Chambersburg PA
CBHW010938140726
47988CB00010B/3507
9798868934995